VISUAL DICTIONARY

NEW EDITION

Ice-silver hair

Cybernetic eye

Titanium
Dragon motif

Titanium arms

TITANIUM ZANE

Whipping tail

Fire-breathing jaws

Chains to control
the dragon

FIRSTBOURNE

LEGO NINJAGO
Masters of Spinjitzu

VISUAL DICTIONARY
NEW EDITION

Sharp fangs on
the wings

Hammer

Written by Arie Kaplan and Hannah Dolan

Cole attached to Firstbourne's foot

CONTENTS

INTRODUCTION

"Ninja-Go!" That's the battle cry of the young ninja in the LEGO® NINJAGO® theme. From the moment Kai, Jay, Cole, and Zane shouted those words in 2011, in both LEGO sets and the LEGO NINJAGO: *Masters of Spinjitzu* TV series, the LEGO NINJAGO theme has proven hugely popular. So much so, that it has spawned ten seasons of the TV series, a 2017 feature film—THE LEGO® NINJAGO® MOVIE™—and a series of video games. Along the way, several new characters have joined Master Wu's team to help fight his many new enemies!

There is never a dull moment in the world of LEGO Ninjago. This action-packed line is all about the battle between good and evil—whether that is the ninja versus a power-mad tyrant called Lord Garmadon, The Skulkins from the Underworld, warring tribes of angry Serpentine,

Morro and his creepy ghost army, a biker gang called the Sons of Garmadon, or the savage Dragon Hunters. The theme even has an all-action game, LEGO NINJAGO: *Spinjitzu Spinners*, which sees your LEGO NINJAGO minifigures go head-to-head aboard whirling spinners.

What captures fans' imaginations most is the NINJAGO characters. Master Wu and each member of his team of ninja recruits has a distinctive personality, but they all have wisdom, warmth, and humor to spare. They always try to choose the best path, but they are also flawed. Seeing the ninja develop is what gives the LEGO NINJAGO theme real heart—their story of learning to do the right thing applies to each and every one of us.

DATA BOXES

Throughout the book, each LEGO NINJAGO set is identified with a data file, which provides the official name of the set, the year of first release, the LEGO identification number of the set, the number of LEGO pieces—or elements— in the set, and the number of minifigures in the set.

Set name
Kai's Blade Cycle & Zane's Snowmobile
Year 2019
Number 70667
Pieces 376
Minifigures 4

TIMELINE

LEGO® NINJAGO® was born in 2011 when the pilot episodes of LEGO NINJAGO: *Masters of Spinjitzu* were broadcast and the first sets of spinners, models, and trading cards were released. Since then, the NINJAGO world has expanded to include further TV seasons, new characters, video games, a movie, and even a theme park ride.

2011

TV PILOT EPISODES

The first pilot episode of the television series LEGO NINJAGO: *Masters of Spinjitzu* is broadcast

KAI (SET 2111)

The first NINJAGO Spinner Set is released

NINJA AMBUSH (2258)

The "Masters of Spinjitzu" sets are released

LEGO BATTLES: NINJAGO

The first NINJAGO video game is released, on the Nintendo DS platform

SEASON 1 (RISE OF THE SNAKES)

The first full season of LEGO NINJAGO: *Masters of Spinjitzu* is broadcast

VENOMARI SHRINE (9440)

The "Rise of the Snakes" sets are released

2012

SEASON 2 (LEGACY OF THE GREEN NINJA)

Season 2 of LEGO NINJAGO: *Masters of Spinjitzu* is broadcast

2013

KAI'S FIRE MECH (70500)

"The Final Battle" sets are released

2014

SEASON 3 (REBOOTED)

Season 3 of LEGO NINJAGO: *Masters of Spinjitzu* is broadcast

HOVER HUNTER (70720)

The "Rebooted" theme sets are released

NINJACOPTER (70724)

This is the first set to include a P.I.X.A.L. minifigure

2015

AIRJITZU KAI FLYER (70739)

The first Airjitzu set is released

SEASON 4 (TOURNAMENT OF ELEMENTS)

Season 4 of LEGO NINJAGO: *Masters of Spinjitzu* is broadcast

ANACONDRAI CRUSHER (70745)

The "Tournament of Elements" sets are released

CONDRAI COPTER ATTACK (70746)

This set features the first appearance of Skylor

SEASON 5 (POSSESSION)

Season 5 of LEGO NINJAGO: *Masters of Spinjitzu* is broadcast

TEMPLE OF AIRJITZU (70751)

The "Possession" sets are released

SEASON 6 (SKYBOUND)

Season 6 of LEGO NINJAGO: *Masters of Spinjitzu* is broadcast

KRYPTARIUM PRISON BREAKOUT (70591)

The "Skybound" sets are released

LEGOLAND RIDE

LEGO NINJAGO—The Ride opens at the LEGOLAND® theme park in California

DAY OF THE DEPARTED

A LEGO NINJAGO: *Masters of Spinjitzu* TV special airs between Seasons 6 and 7

TITANIUM NINJA TUMBLER (70588)

The "Day of the Departed" sets are released

2017

SEASON 7 (THE HANDS OF TIME)

Season 7 of LEGO NINJAGO: *Masters of Spinjitzu* is broadcast

VERMILLION ATTACK (70621)

"The Hands of Time" sets are released

FEATURE FILM

THE LEGO® NINJAGO® MOVIE™ opens. It is the first theatrical feature film involving the Ninjago characters

MASTER FALLS (70608)

THE LEGO NINJAGO MOVIE sets are released

LEGO NINJAGO MOVIE VIDEO GAME

The movie tie-in video game is released, on PS4, Xbox One, Nintendo Switch, and Windows PC platforms

NINJAGO® CITY (70620)

This becomes the largest LEGO NINJAGO set released to date, with 4,867 pieces

2018

SEASON 8 (SONS OF GARMADON)

Season 8 of LEGO NINJAGO: *Masters of Spinjitzu* is broadcast. It features a new style of animation first seen in THE LEGO NINJAGO MOVIE

KATANA VII (70638)

The "Sons of Garmadon" sets are released

SEASON 9 (HUNTED)

Season 9 of LEGO NINJAGO: *Masters of Spinjitzu* is broadcast

DESTINY'S WING (70650)

The "Hunted" sets are released

KAI—SPINJITZU MASTER (70633)

The first Spinjitzu Masters set is released

GOLDEN DRAGON MASTER (70644)

The first Dragon Masters set is released

2019

SAMURAI MECH (70665)

The "Legacy" sets are released

SEASON 10 (MARCH OF THE ONI)

Season 10 of LEGO NINJAGO: *Masters of Spinjitzu* is broadcast

CHAPTER 1:
FRIENDS

Robe color matches his eyes

LLOYD

The son of super villain Lord Garmadon, Lloyd at first wishes to follow in his father's footsteps. Lloyd finds a better purpose when his uncle, Master Wu, takes him under his wing. Through Wu's guidance and the friendship of the other ninja, Lloyd sets out on the path to becoming the Ultimate Spinjitzu Master. Along the way, he discovers his true destiny as the Green Ninja and a Ninjago hero.

TINY TROUBLE

Young Lloyd dresses in a black hooded cloak to appear tougher. Young Lloyd accidentally takes command of an evil snake tribe.

▲ LEGACY LLOYD

Lloyd is battle ready in his 2019 robes, an updated version of the original ninja robes, known as gi. The emblem on his torso is a symbol of his Elemental Dragon. Lloyd's green eyes indicate that his powers have been unlocked.

Windswept hair

Exhaust pipe

Steering control

Golden side blade

Low suspension

◀ LLOYD'S MOTORBIKE

Techno Lloyd knows that a compact motorcycle is the best form of transportation for whizzing around the narrow streets of Ninjago City. The bike's speed is especially helpful when the traffic takes the form of an army of Nindroid soldiers determined to destroy the busy metropolis!

Set name	*Overborg Attack*	
Year 2014		**Number** 70722
Pieces 207		**Minifigures** 2

Gold shoulder armor

LLOYD ZX

The goal of all of Wu's ninja trainees is to wear the emerald robes of the legendary Green Ninja. But it is only Lloyd's destiny to do so.

TECHNO LLOYD

Lloyd briefly becomes the Golden Ninja. He soon returns to his green robes, but still has the potential to become the Ultimate Spinjitzu Master.

Brow knitted in concentration

LLOYD DESTINY

Lloyd dons new robes to study a tornado-themed martial arts technique called Airjitzu. He is now ready to battle a crew of dastardly Sky Pirates.

WEAPONS

Lloyd's weapon of choice is a simple katana sword. He is also skilled with weapons of all shapes and sizes, from little to large.

SHURIKEN   GOLDEN KATANA   STAFF

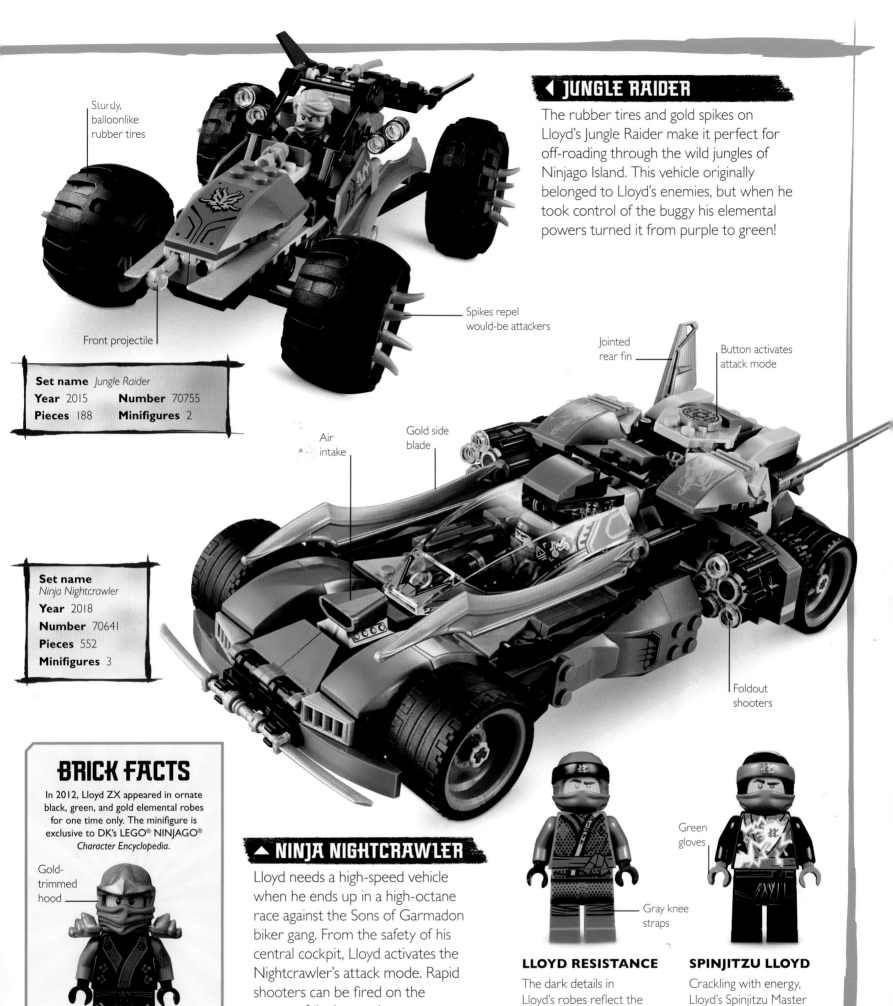

◀ JUNGLE RAIDER

The rubber tires and gold spikes on Lloyd's Jungle Raider make it perfect for off-roading through the wild jungles of Ninjago Island. This vehicle originally belonged to Lloyd's enemies, but when he took control of the buggy his elemental powers turned it from purple to green!

Sturdy, balloonlike rubber tires

Front projectile

Spikes repel would-be attackers

Set name *Jungle Raider*
Year 2015   **Number** 70755
Pieces 188   **Minifigures** 2

Jointed rear fin

Button activates attack mode

Air intake

Gold side blade

Set name
Ninja Nightcrawler
Year 2018
Number 70641
Pieces 552
Minifigures 3

Foldout shooters

BRICK FACTS

In 2012, Lloyd ZX appeared in ornate black, green, and gold elemental robes for one time only. The minifigure is exclusive to DK's LEGO® NINJAGO® *Character Encyclopedia*.

Gold-trimmed hood

▲ NINJA NIGHTCRAWLER

Lloyd needs a high-speed vehicle when he ends up in a high-octane race against the Sons of Garmadon biker gang. From the safety of his central cockpit, Lloyd activates the Nightcrawler's attack mode. Rapid shooters can be fired on the go—useful when trying to prevent his speedy enemies from reuniting the dangerous Oni Masks.

Green gloves

Gray knee straps

LLOYD RESISTANCE

The dark details in Lloyd's robes reflect the seriousness with which he regards his new responsibilities, as he becomes "Master Lloyd."

SPINJITZU LLOYD

Crackling with energy, Lloyd's Spinjitzu Master outfit is a typical training gi, with a twist. It's practically bursting with his explosive elemental power!

GOLDEN DRAGON

When Lloyd briefly becomes the Golden Ninja, one of his enhanced ninja skills is the ability to summon a Golden Dragon made of pure light energy. Lloyd and the impressive dragon use Golden Power to hurl bursts of energy at their enemies, including the Stone Army and the Overlord. After the Golden Dragon is no longer needed, it disappears into the air until next called upon.

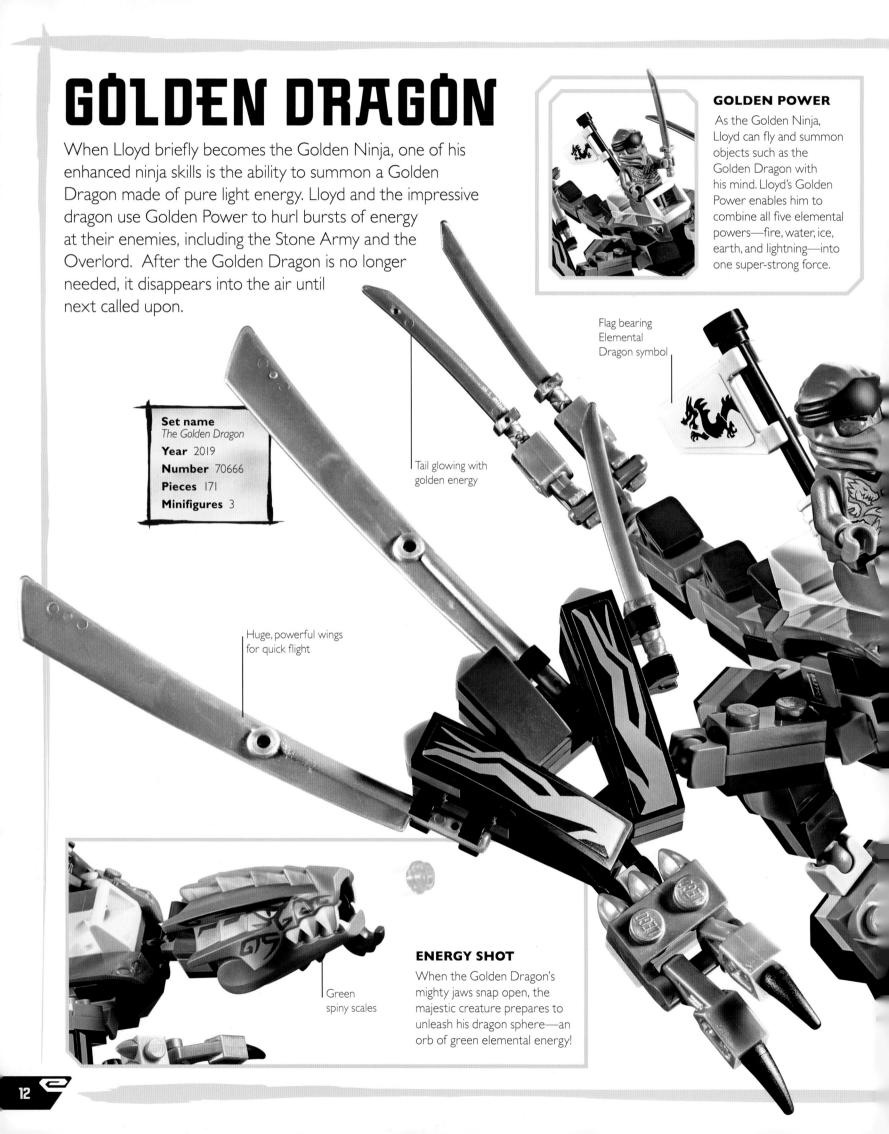

GOLDEN POWER

As the Golden Ninja, Lloyd can fly and summon objects such as the Golden Dragon with his mind. Lloyd's Golden Power enables him to combine all five elemental powers—fire, water, ice, earth, and lightning—into one super-strong force.

Set name
The Golden Dragon
Year 2019
Number 70666
Pieces 171
Minifigures 3

Tail glowing with golden energy

Flag bearing Elemental Dragon symbol

Huge, powerful wings for quick flight

Green spiny scales

ENERGY SHOT

When the Golden Dragon's mighty jaws snap open, the majestic creature prepares to unleash his dragon sphere—an orb of green elemental energy!

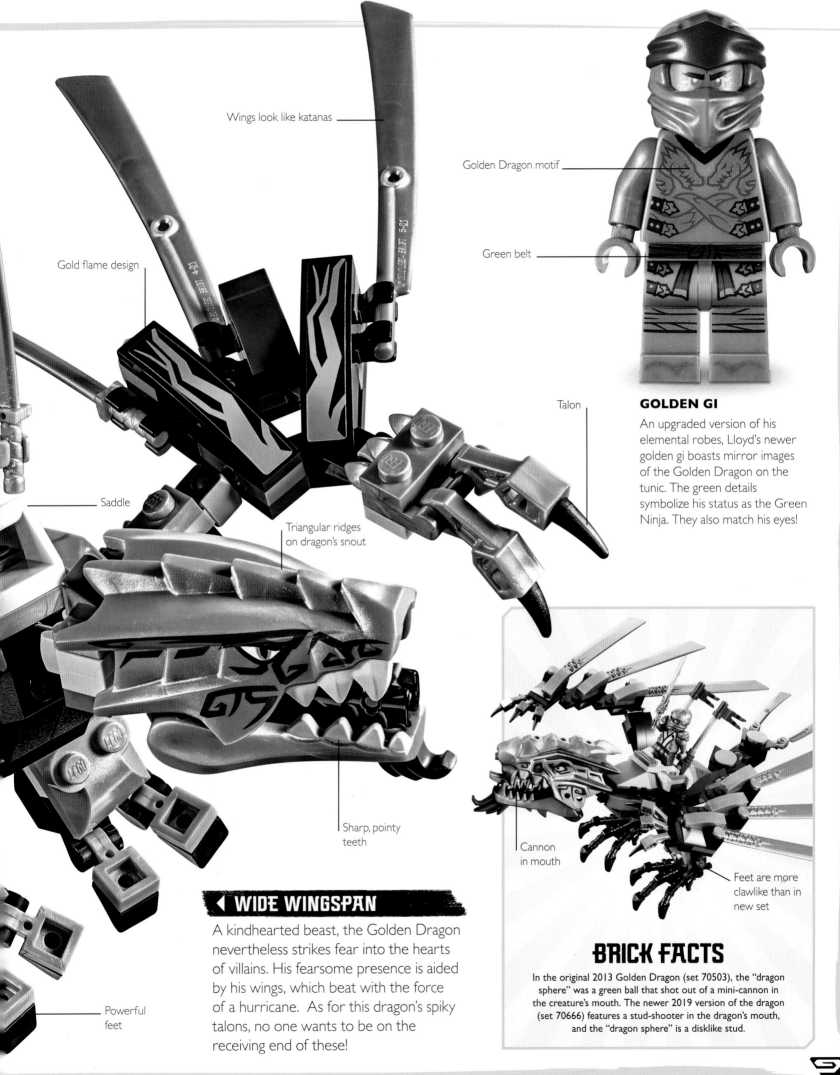

Wings look like katanas

Golden Dragon motif

Green belt

Gold flame design

Saddle

Triangular ridges on dragon's snout

Talon

GOLDEN GI

An upgraded version of his elemental robes, Lloyd's newer golden gi boasts mirror images of the Golden Dragon on the tunic. The green details symbolize his status as the Green Ninja. They also match his eyes!

Sharp, pointy teeth

Cannon in mouth

Feet are more clawlike than in new set

◀ WIDE WINGSPAN

A kindhearted beast, the Golden Dragon nevertheless strikes fear into the hearts of villains. His fearsome presence is aided by his wings, which beat with the force of a hurricane. As for this dragon's spiky talons, no one wants to be on the receiving end of these!

Powerful feet

BRICK FACTS

In the original 2013 Golden Dragon (set 70503), the "dragon sphere" was a green ball that shot out of a mini-cannon in the creature's mouth. The newer 2019 version of the dragon (set 70666) features a stud-shooter in the dragon's mouth, and the "dragon sphere" is a disklike stud.

Gold designs on robes

MASTER WU

Master Wu is the son of the First Spinjitzu Master, who created the Ninjago world using the four Golden Weapons. Since his father's death, Wu has devoted his life to a single purpose: protecting Ninjago from destructive forces, including his evil older brother, Lord Garmadon. A strong and skilled Spinjitzu Master, Wu is a firm but fair mentor to his trainee ninja. However, when Wu is accidentally de-aged in a Time Blade, it is up to the ninja to look after young Wu!

▲ TEMPLE WU

No one knows how old Wu is, but his long white beard shows that he has lived for many years. He makes the peaceful Temple of Airjitzu his part-time base of operations. When Wu strolls around the temple and visits its tea shop, he wears ornately detailed robes and plans for his retirement.

WISE TEACHER

Wu wears a kimono to train his ninja students in the battle skills he has learned over a lifetime as a Spinjitzu Master.

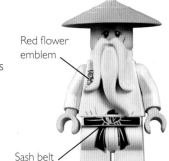

Red flower emblem

Sash belt

Hot-air balloon

◀ WU'S BALLOON

Wu normally relies on his mastery of martial arts to fight enemies. However, when the Sky Pirates attack the ninja, Master Wu fights back from above in his hot-air balloon. It may be small, but this micro-airship has fast rotor blades. The craft is also perfect for dropping coconuts on the heads of the invading pirates!

Rotor blades

Basket

Set name
Tiger Widow Island
Year 2016
Number 70604
Pieces 450
Minifigures 5

Cyborg parts implanted by the Overlord

Silver hat

◀ EVIL WU

Even Master Wu cannot always escape the bad guys. Poor Wu is captured by the villainous Digital Overlord. The Overlord uses his technology to turn Wu into a cyborg named Evil Wu. The ninja recognize their teacher, despite his black beard and robotic eye.

BLACK OUTFIT

Wu isn't always dressed in white—he also wears an elaborate black kimono. A long gray scarf adds an elegant touch to his outfit.

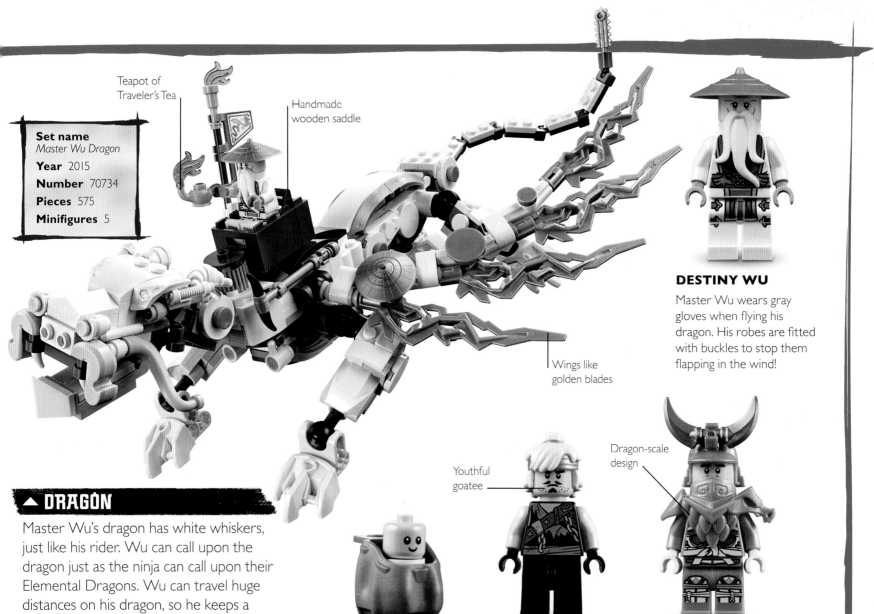

Teapot of
Traveler's Tea

Handmade
wooden saddle

Set name
Master Wu Dragon
Year 2015
Number 70734
Pieces 575
Minifigures 5

Wings like
golden blades

▲ DRAGON

Master Wu's dragon has white whiskers, just like his rider. Wu can call upon the dragon just as the ninja can call upon their Elemental Dragons. Wu can travel huge distances on his dragon, so he keeps a kettle of Traveler's Tea near the saddle in case he gets thirsty.

DESTINY WU

Master Wu wears gray gloves when flying his dragon. His robes are fitted with buckles to stop them flapping in the wind!

Youthful
goatee

Dragon-scale
design

BABY WU

The ninja are shocked when they discover their teacher has been turned into a baby by the Reversal Time Blade. Luckily, the wise Spinjitzu Master ages quickly, so his students aren't on diaper duty for long!

TEEN WU

Wu is soon a supercool teenager, with a stylish haircut and stubble on his chin. His scruffy robes are the result of his encounters with the Iron Baron and the rest of the Dragon Hunters gang.

DRAGON MASTER

Teenage Wu finds the Dragon Armor—special golden armor created by the Firstbourne dragon and Wu's father, the first Spinjitzu Master. Wu uses it to battle his brother, Garmadon.

BRICK FACTS

This book comes with an exclusive Master Wu minifigure, in his teenage state. When he is de-aged, Master Wu has to relearn many of his old skills. This minifigure is wearing Spinjitzu training robes.

▶ TRAINING GROUND

When the ninja practice their skills, they sometimes use a training dummy that looks like Master Wu. The dummy even has two sai to defend itself. However, this dummy is more easily defeated than the formidable Master Wu himself!

Golden sai

Set name *Master's Training Grounds*
Year 2017   **Number** 30425
Pieces 43   **Minifigures** 2

Pouches for essential items

KAI

Fire Ninja Kai has always had fire in his blood. Wise Master Wu discovered this headstrong hero when Kai was running his late father's blacksmith shop. Wu saw a spark in him, and recruited him to complete his ninja team. Kai has had to work hard to control his hot temper. Once he learns to master his emotions, he becomes a truly unstoppable force.

▼ BLADE CYCLE

Kai blazes across Ninjago on this Blade Cycle. If its super speed does not frighten Serpentine enemies, its big blade attack function will. When enemies strike, the sides of Kai's cycle open up and four hidden katana swords pop out for a sharp defense!

Hood

Gold wheel rim

Set name	
Kai's Blade Cycle & Zane's Snowmobile	
Year	2019
Number	70667
Pieces	376
Minifigures	4

▲ KAI FS

Ever since he first embarked on his ninja training, Kai has preferred to wear robes in his trademark fiery red. When he uses the power of Forbidden Spinjtzu, his elemental power is released as energy from his mind. Mess with the Fire Ninja and you will get burned!

Set name	
Katana V11	
Year	2018
Number	70638
Pieces	257
Minifigures	2

◄ KATANA VII

When Kai needs to rescue Lloyd from the Sons of Garmadon, he jumps in the cockpit of his stealthy Katana VII boat. Sensing trouble, Kai puts the Katana VII in attack mode. Pods pop out at either side, ready to launch shooters and help Kai free his friend.

Pods with shooters

Sharp front blades

KAI DX

Dragon taming is no problem for Kai. He is the first of the ninja to achieve DX (Dragon eXtreme) ninja status when he learns to control the deadly Fire Dragon. He is proud to wear his new dragon-emblazoned DX robes.

Set name *Kai Fighter*
Year 2014
Number 70721
Pieces 196
Minifigures 2

Twin front blades

Golden missile, ready to fire

"Flame Dragon" emblem

Symbols spell "fire"

◀ KAI'S FIGHTER

For a full-blown aerial assault, Kai hops into the cockpit of this Fighter plane. It was once an ordinary civilian aircraft, but Techno Kai transformed it into a Fighter fit for a ninja using his powerful Techno-Blade. The Fire Ninja's Nindroid enemies had better take cover—Kai's Fighter has the power to fire golden missiles, and it never misses!

NRG KAI

Kai has never looked hotter than when he unlocks his True Potential! His eyes glow and his kimono is covered in blasts of red-hot energy.

GOLDEN KAI

While in the Digiverse, all the ninja can access the power of the Gold Ninja. Kai struggles to overcome his fear, but when he does he is embraced by the Golden Power!

DEEPSTONE ARMOR KAI

Master Wu gives the ninja these outfits to fight ghosts. They have shoulder armor made of Deepstone, which is harmful to ghosts.

KAI HONOR

Kai wears these robes when he thinks about his past during the Day of the Departed. They are a mix of his Original Ninja, ZX, and Deepstone outfits.

KAI RESISTANCE

Kai has an unusually cautious face when he battles the Sons of Garmadon. The "cross" on his robes shows he sometimes feels he's at a crossroads in life.

▼ KAI'S CHARGER

When the ninja take on technologically advanced enemies such as Nindroids, they must fight back with equally advanced vehicles. Kai's Charger has a built-in surprise for the Nindroids—its hood lifts up to reveal a motorcycle at its core. Kai can roar away on it if he finds his enemies are getting too close.

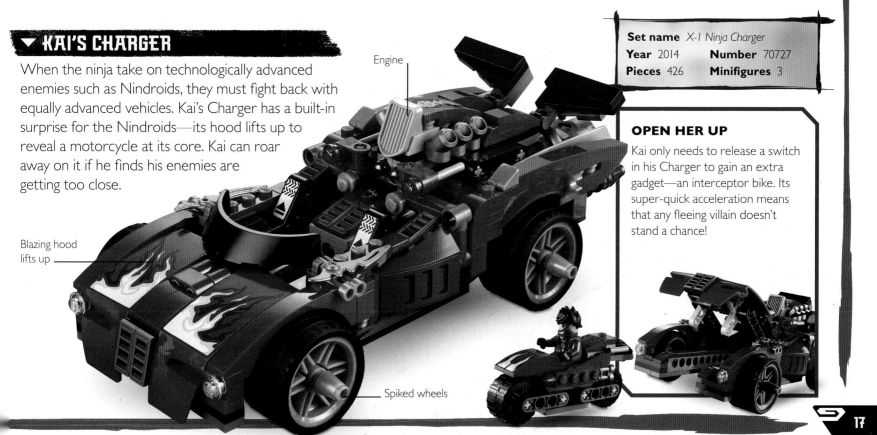

Blazing hood lifts up

Engine

Spiked wheels

Set name *X-1 Ninja Charger*
Year 2014 **Number** 70727
Pieces 426 **Minifigures** 3

OPEN HER UP

Kai only needs to release a switch in his Charger to gain an extra gadget—an interceptor bike. Its super-quick acceleration means that any fleeing villain doesn't stand a chance!

NINJA FAMILY

Kai and Nya, the Elemental Masters of Fire and Water, have many differences. One thing they share, however, is family. The siblings grew up together in a blacksmith shop, after their parents' mysterious disappearance. Nya and Kai discover their mom and dad are being held captive. They will have to work together to rescue their parents!

BLADE BRAVERY

Only by working together can Kai and Nya help their parents, so they both grab the Dragon Dagger. The weapon features blades in red and blue—the colors of the Fire and Water Ninja.

▼ DRAGON'S FORGE

Kai and Nya's parents, Ray and Maya, are being held captive in the Dragon's Forge blacksmith shop. They're being forced to make weapons for their enemies! The ninja siblings have to free their parents, but they first need to fight their way past a sea of foes.

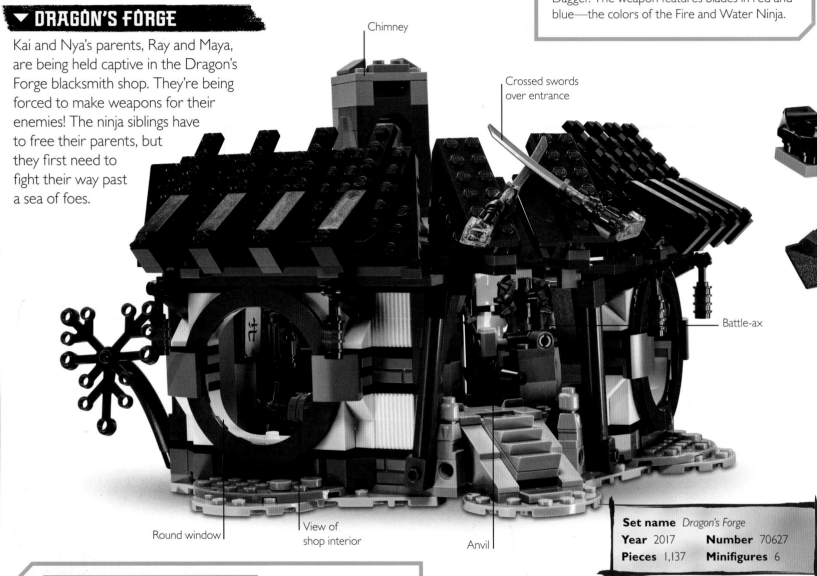

Chimney

Crossed swords over entrance

Battle-ax

Round window

View of shop interior

Anvil

Set name	*Dragon's Forge*		
Year	2017	**Number**	70627
Pieces	1,137	**Minifigures**	6

RAY'S DISMAY

The blacksmith shop where Ray and Maya are being held resembles a shop they used to run called Four Weapons. As Ray inspects a recently forged weapon, he hopes that he and his wife will soon be free.

Hair is spiky, like Kai's

Dragon head emblem

RAY

Ray was the Elemental Master of Fire before his son stepped into the role. In his younger days, Ray fought alongside Master Wu in many battles, and they became close friends.

Two tails provide
double the power

Kai stands
behind Nya

Extended wings

▲ FUSION DRAGON

The Fusion Dragon is a mixture
of the ninja's powers of Fire and
Water. It is summoned by Kai and
Nya when they concentrate their
powers and work together.

Red front
claw

Snapping jaws

Blue headband
for Water Ninja

Shoulder armor

Blacksmith's
apron

Reversal
Time Blade

MAYA

Maya used to be the Master of
Water, a role now taken up by
her daughter. Maya fought with
the other Elemental Masters in the
Serpentine War before cofounding
the Four Weapons blacksmith shop.

NYA

Nya is dressed in a version of
her ninja robes, complete with
protective outer panels. The
scroll pattern at her neck is
reminiscent of the decoration
on her mother's outfit.

KAI

Kai's eyes crackle with fiery
red elemental energy as he
tries to free his parents
from their captors. He
wields the powerful
Reversal Time Blade.

Determined face

Blue kneepad

NYA

Nya is a talented engineer. She uses both her intelligence and fierce fighting skills in battle. As Kai's little sister, she originally chooses to forge her own path by going undercover as the mysterious warrior Samurai X. She later embraces her destiny as the Water Ninja.

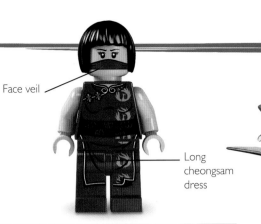

Face veil

Long cheongsam dress

▲ TRAINING NYA

The gold pattern on Nya's dress looks very similar to the emblem of the mysterious Samurai X. The red fabric also connects her to her protective brother Kai, the Fire Ninja. However, tough Nya soon proves she can hold her own in any situation.

▲ NYA HUNTED

When the Sons of Garmadon biker gang try to enforce Lord Garmadon's rule in Ninjago City, Nya and Lloyd lead a resistance force to fight the tyranny. The blue on Nya's robes symbolizes her status as the Water Ninja.

Samurai X flag

Projectile launcher

Hinged cockpit area

Large katana

Set name
The Samurai Mech
Year 2019
Number 70665
Pieces 154
Minifigures 3

Gold, hornlike crest

Metal torso shield

NYA SAMURAI X

As her alter ego, Samurai X, Nya hides all but her determined stare behind a handmade Samurai outfit.

Face mask conceals her identity

▶ SAMURAI MECH

In Samurai X guise, Nya uses the Samurai Mech on dangerous missions such as battling the Serpentine. It's armed with projectile launchers, a huge katana, and a net. Instead of a left hand, the giant robot suit has two backup swords.

Twin swords

JUNGLE SAMURAI X 3.0

When the other ninja compete in the Tournament of Elements, Nya uses her Samurai X armor to spy on their opponents.

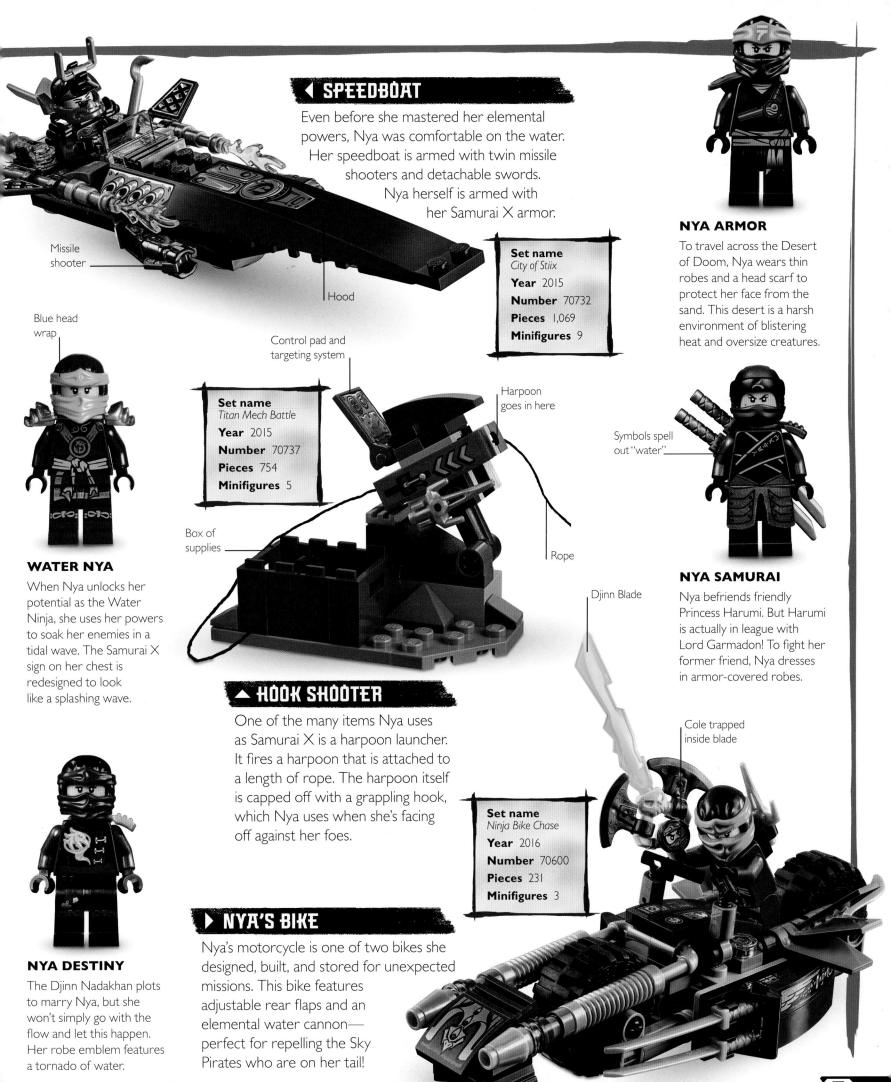

◀ SPEEDBOAT

Even before she mastered her elemental powers, Nya was comfortable on the water. Her speedboat is armed with twin missile shooters and detachable swords. Nya herself is armed with her Samurai X armor.

Missile shooter

Hood

Set name *City of Stiix*
Year 2015
Number 70732
Pieces 1,069
Minifigures 9

NYA ARMOR

To travel across the Desert of Doom, Nya wears thin robes and a head scarf to protect her face from the sand. This desert is a harsh environment of blistering heat and oversize creatures.

Blue head wrap

Control pad and targeting system

Harpoon goes in here

Set name *Titan Mech Battle*
Year 2015
Number 70737
Pieces 754
Minifigures 5

Box of supplies

Rope

WATER NYA

When Nya unlocks her potential as the Water Ninja, she uses her powers to soak her enemies in a tidal wave. The Samurai X sign on her chest is redesigned to look like a splashing wave.

Symbols spell out "water"

NYA SAMURAI

Nya befriends friendly Princess Harumi. But Harumi is actually in league with Lord Garmadon! To fight her former friend, Nya dresses in armor-covered robes.

▲ HOOK SHOOTER

One of the many items Nya uses as Samurai X is a harpoon launcher. It fires a harpoon that is attached to a length of rope. The harpoon itself is capped off with a grappling hook, which Nya uses when she's facing off against her foes.

Djinn Blade

Cole trapped inside blade

Set name *Ninja Bike Chase*
Year 2016
Number 70600
Pieces 231
Minifigures 3

▶ NYA'S BIKE

Nya's motorcycle is one of two bikes she designed, built, and stored for unexpected missions. This bike features adjustable rear flaps and an elemental water cannon—perfect for repelling the Sky Pirates who are on her tail!

NYA DESTINY

The Djinn Nadakhan plots to marry Nya, but she won't simply go with the flow and let this happen. Her robe emblem features a tornado of water.

SAMURAI X CAVE

Deep in the desert, behind an abandoned dragon's skull, lies the secret entrance to a cleverly concealed ninja hideout. The cave's rocky walls disguise a high-tech lab where the ninja can build jets, track their enemies' movements, and store their gadgets for safekeeping. The cave originally stored Nya's secret Samurai X equipment, but she has since shared the cave's secrets with her fellow ninja.

LASER PRISON
The cave's prison cell has laser "bars" to trap the trespassers safely inside. Just in case the villains try to escape, a guard robot keeps watch from its perch directly above the cell.

Stone Army swordsman

Protective armor

Nya

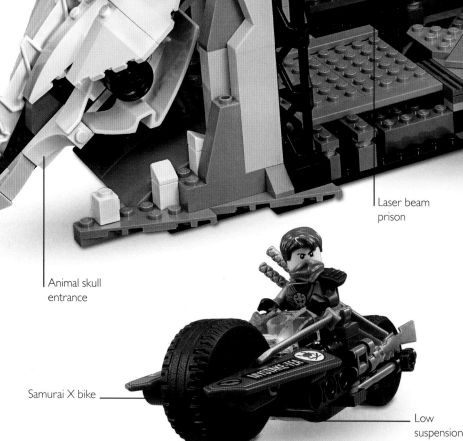

Laser beam prison

Animal skull entrance

Samurai X bike

Low suspension

SAMURAI X MECH
Hopping into the cockpit of this imposing mech, Nya faces off against invaders. The mech has a blade jutting out of each forearm and a sai in each fist. Nya can even attach a device to the armored mech to make it take off and fly! This tall machine is truly designed to make short work of enemy trespassers.

Set name	Samurai X Cave Chaos	
Year	2016	**Number** 70596
Pieces	1,253	**Minifigures** 8

Nose cone of
jet plane

Rotors for
upward flight

GOING UP

As the ninja's resident
mechanic and inventor,
Nya has built a functioning
elevator, which can deposit
her in the mech. It can
also take the ninja to
the surface to face
their adversaries!

Jet launchpad

Master Wu
operates control pad

Elevator controls

Safety warning
lights

▲ ULTIMATE DEFENSE

The cave is a treasure trove of gadgets.
At the touch of a button, the launch pad
splits apart. The left side reveals a hidden
stash of weapons. The right side takes Nya
closer to her Samurai X armor. Meanwhile,
overhead screens give the ninja information
on their attackers' whereabouts.

Determined look in his eyes

Knotted belt

JAY

Lightning Ninja Jay is a real bright spark. He loves to invent new gadgets and gizmos, even if they don't always work out as he plans. Jay also has a lightning-fast wit but, unfortunately, it is mostly only Jay who finds his jokes funny! He might be the most lighthearted of the ninja, but Jay takes his ninja training very seriously. He works hard to hone his battle skills so he can strike down any enemies who threaten Ninjago.

TRAINING JAY

When Master Wu spotted Jay trying out some mechanical wings he had invented, Wu saw a spark of genius in him. Jay agreed to leave his parents' junkyard home and begin training with Wu as the blue-robed Lightning Ninja.

▲ SPINJITZU JAY

Jay is a talented warrior. In fact, he is the first to master the art of Spinjitzu. When he achieves the rank of Spinjitzu Master, Jay receives robes that crackle with elemental lightning power!

Hinged wing tips are adjustable

Aerodynamic rear fins

Removable shield

Jay in the cockpit

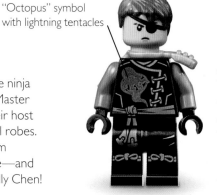

Flight deck

Set name
Jay's Storm Fighter
Year 2019
Number 70668
Pieces 490
Minifigures 4

▲ STORM FIGHTER

When Jay's Storm Fighter emerges from the clouds like a lightning bolt, it is best to take cover! This fast fighter jet is built for air-to-air combat. If Jay spots an enemy aircraft, the wings on his Storm Fighter extend to reveal hidden ninja swords.

Metal armor worn over one arm

JAY ZX

A lightning-fast learner, Jay is quick to master new techniques. When he reaches the ZX (Zen eXtreme) level of his ninja training, Jay is faster than ever in combat, especially when piloting his Storm Fighter.

Pouch holds weapons

"Octopus" symbol with lightning tentacles

JUNGLE JAY

When Jay and the ninja were invited to Master Chen's island, their host gave them special robes. They helped them survive the jungle—and to defeat dastardly Chen!

JAY DESTINY

When Jay is held captive on the Sky Pirate ship *Misfortune's Keep*, he faces off against the crew. He loses that battle and briefly wears an eyepatch to cover his wounds.

▶ THUNDER RAIDER

Inventive Jay puts his mechanical skills to use by packing the ninja vehicles with hidden features and weapons. Jay's Thunder Raider is not only filled with concealed missiles—it can also combine with Cole's Earth Mech to create a doubly-dangerous monster machine.

Techno Jay in the cockpit

Cole's Earth Mech attaches here

High-grip front treads

Roaring rear tires

Set name	*Thunder Raider*	
Year 2014	**Number** 70723	
Pieces 334	**Minifigures** 3	

▼ DESERT LIGHTNING BIKE

Jay's foster father created this mega-fast motorcycle. Jay uses the bike to snatch the Slow-Motion Blade from the villainous Vermillion before they can use it to slow down time! When they attack Jay, he activates the bike's lightning boosters and the attackers are thrown off.

Lightning-blue exhaust flame

Muffler capped with golden blade

Aeroblade

JAY DEEPSTONE

After the villainous ghost Morro opens a bridge between the Cursed Realm and Ninjago, Jay suits up with ghost-hunting equipment. If his Lightning Pack can't get rid of the ghosts, his Aeroblade certainly can!

Holding tank

Jay gripping his Lightning Pack

Set name	*Desert Lightning*	
Year 2017	**Number** 70622	
Pieces 201	**Minifigures** 3	

▶ JAY WALKER ONE

This truck was designed by the ninja's old ally, Cyrus Borg, who created it to fight ghosts who were threatening Ninjago. This vehicle's main weapon is a cannon that sucks up ghouls and spirits and puts them in a holding tank in the rear.

Strong, bulky tires

Set name	*Jay Walker One*	
Year 2015	**Number** 70731	
Pieces 386	**Minifigures** 4	

ZANE

Ice Ninja Zane has always been unusual. When Master Wu first met him, he was meditating at the bottom of a frozen pond! Zane has some strange habits and does not always understand jokes, which makes it difficult for him to fit in with a wisecracking team of ninja trainees. However, when Zane learns to accept his differences and sees that he will always receive a warm welcome from Master Wu and the other ninja, the Ice Ninja begins to melt—and unlocks his True Potential.

Letter "Z" in the Ninjago alphabet

▼ ZANE'S SNOWMOBILE

A master of his element, Zane has vehicles at his disposal that can skid across snow and ice at super speed. Zane's Snowmobile has a solid ice exterior that can withstand any impact.

Hood with ice-themed detailing

▲ ZANE ARMOR

When the ninja learn of the Scrolls of Forbidden Spinjitzu, Zane has a terrible dream about his destiny. Zane's nightmare comes true and he finds himself blasted into the icy Ever-Realm, where time works differently. To get home, Zane must face his toughest test yet.

Ski-style blade

Missile shooter

Set name	Kai's Blade Cycle & Zane's Snowmobile	
Year	2019	Number 70667
Pieces	376	Minifigures 4

TRAINING ZANE

When Zane becomes Master Wu's ninja recruit, he is an orphan with no memory of his past. Polite and respectful, Zane is proud to wear the white robes of the Ice Ninja.

NRG ZANE

When Zane discovers the truth about his past and learns to accept who he really is, he unlocks his True Potential—and becomes a chillingly powerful NRG Ninja.

ZANE RX

Zane is a Nindroid—a powerful mechanical being created by his inventor father. When he is scarred in battle, Zane's metal body parts and switches are exposed.

ECHO ZANE

Echo Zane is a replica of Zane built by his creator, Dr. Julien. However, Echo Zane is prone to rust and damage. The rusty robot helps Jay rescue Nya and the other ninja from the Sky Pirates.

Rusty color

BRICK FACTS

The 2014 edition of DK's LEGO® NINJAGO® *Visual Dictionary* came with a limited-edition Zane minifigure. Zane's robes are wrapped with a silver sash and feature an ice element symbol surrounded by pulsing ice energy. He also has his signature flattop hairstyle on show.

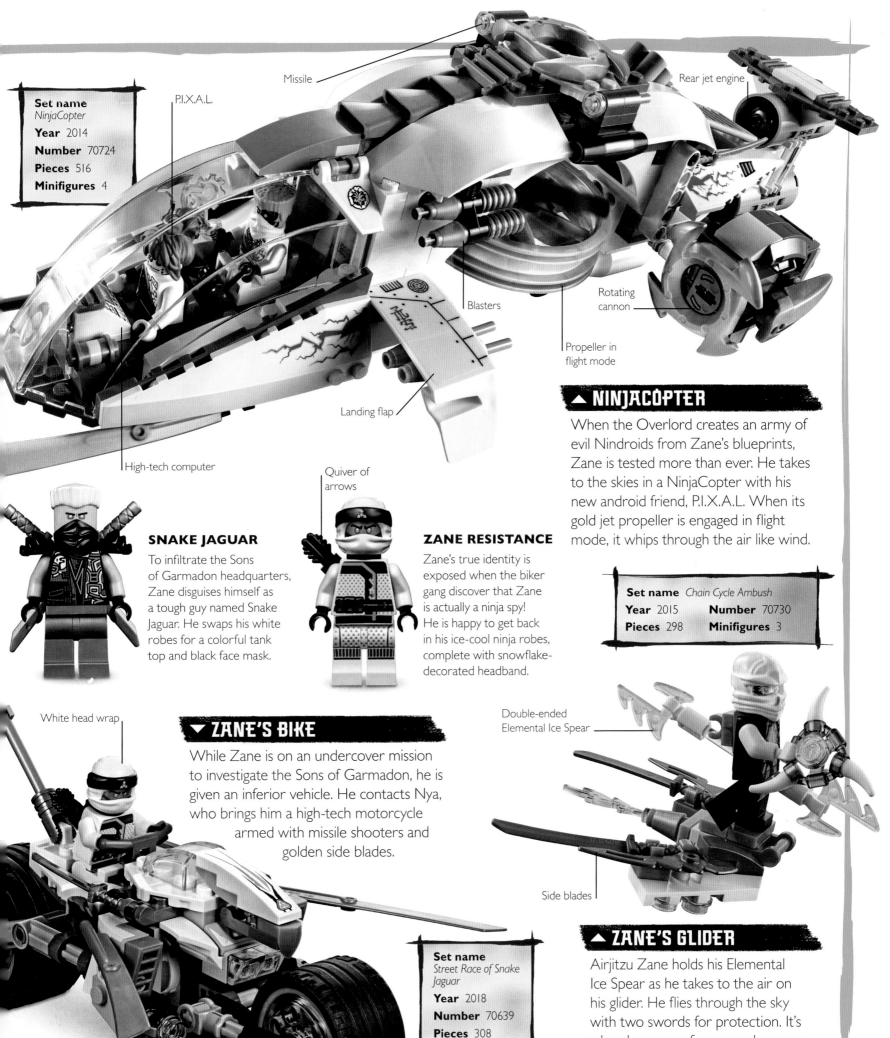

Set name *NinjaCopter*
Year 2014
Number 70724
Pieces 516
Minifigures 4

Missile

P.I.X.A.L.

Rear jet engine

Blasters

Rotating cannon

Propeller in flight mode

Landing flap

High-tech computer

Quiver of arrows

▲ NINJACOPTER

When the Overlord creates an army of evil Nindroids from Zane's blueprints, Zane is tested more than ever. He takes to the skies in a NinjaCopter with his new android friend, P.I.X.A.L. When its gold jet propeller is engaged in flight mode, it whips through the air like wind.

SNAKE JAGUAR

To infiltrate the Sons of Garmadon headquarters, Zane disguises himself as a tough guy named Snake Jaguar. He swaps his white robes for a colorful tank top and black face mask.

ZANE RESISTANCE

Zane's true identity is exposed when the biker gang discover that Zane is actually a ninja spy! He is happy to get back in his ice-cool ninja robes, complete with snowflake-decorated headband.

Set name *Chain Cycle Ambush*
Year 2015   **Number** 70730
Pieces 298   **Minifigures** 3

White head wrap

▼ ZANE'S BIKE

While Zane is on an undercover mission to investigate the Sons of Garmadon, he is given an inferior vehicle. He contacts Nya, who brings him a high-tech motorcycle armed with missile shooters and golden side blades.

Double-ended Elemental Ice Spear

Side blades

Missile shooter

Set name *Street Race of Snake Jaguar*
Year 2018
Number 70639
Pieces 308
Minifigures 2

▲ ZANE'S GLIDER

Airjitzu Zane holds his Elemental Ice Spear as he takes to the air on his glider. He flies through the sky with two swords for protection. It's a handy means of escape when you are being chased by villainous ghosts!

TITANIUM NINJA

When Zane seemingly gives his life to save his friends, the other ninja mourn for their fallen comrade. However, it turns out that Zane has uploaded his Nindroid mind into a computer network and built himself a new body! Shortly afterward, he decides he is no longer the Ice Ninja and instead becomes the Titanium Ninja!

▶ TITANIUM DRAGON

The armor-plated Titanium Dragon is conjured up by Zane out of elemental energy. At first, Zane fears the creature. But when he becomes the Titanium Ninja, Zane confidently rides the dragon.

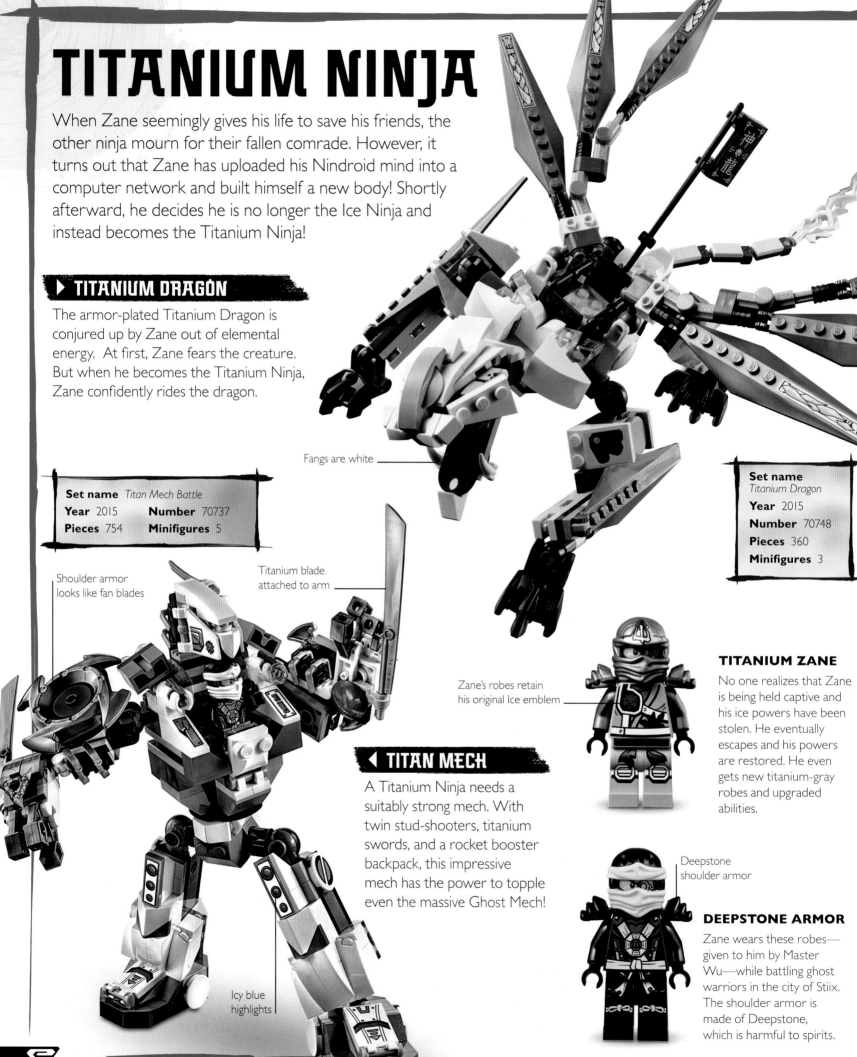

Fangs are white

Set name	Titan Mech Battle	
Year	2015	
Pieces	754	Number 70737
		Minifigures 5

Set name	Titanium Dragon
Year	2015
Number	70748
Pieces	360
Minifigures	3

Shoulder armor looks like fan blades

Titanium blade attached to arm

Zane's robes retain his original Ice emblem

◀ TITAN MECH

A Titanium Ninja needs a suitably strong mech. With twin stud-shooters, titanium swords, and a rocket booster backpack, this impressive mech has the power to topple even the massive Ghost Mech!

Icy blue highlights

TITANIUM ZANE

No one realizes that Zane is being held captive and his ice powers have been stolen. He eventually escapes and his powers are restored. He even gets new titanium-gray robes and upgraded abilities.

Deepstone shoulder armor

DEEPSTONE ARMOR

Zane wears these robes— given to him by Master Wu—while battling ghost warriors in the city of Stiix. The shoulder armor is made of Deepstone, which is harmful to spirits.

HONOR ROBE ZANE

These robes are a mix of the Original Ninja outfits, ZX gi, and Deepstone armor. As such, they represent tradition and honor. The silver details are new additions for the Titanium Ninja.

Silver kneepads

▼ TITANIUM NINJA TUMBLER

Zane zooms across Ninjago in his ice-white tumbler. The vehicle is packed with high-tech features, including missiles, to help Zane against his Nindroid enemies. There's also a prison cell in the back to hold the robotic rogues. If the Nindroids swarm his vehicle, Zane can soar away on the tumbler's detachable flyer.

Wings grow wider during flight

Zane at the controls

Forward-opening cockpit door

Cool "ice" detailing on vehicle

Chunky tires

Hubcaps resemble Master Wu's hat

Set name	Titanium Ninja Tumbler	
Year 2016	**Number** 70588	
Pieces 342	**Minifigures** 3	

BRICK FACTS

The silver "Jungle Zane" robes made their first television appearance at the end of the "Forgotten Elements" episode (season 4, episode 7) of the LEGO NINJAGO: *Masters of Spinjitzu* TV series.

Headband is brown, like earth

Blasts of earth energy

COLE

Earth Ninja Cole has a nature that is as solid and dependable as his element. Cole is always calm and cool-headed—the other ninja tend to look to him in a crisis. His elemental power gives Cole supreme physical and emotional strength. He always puts his strength to the test by challenging himself.

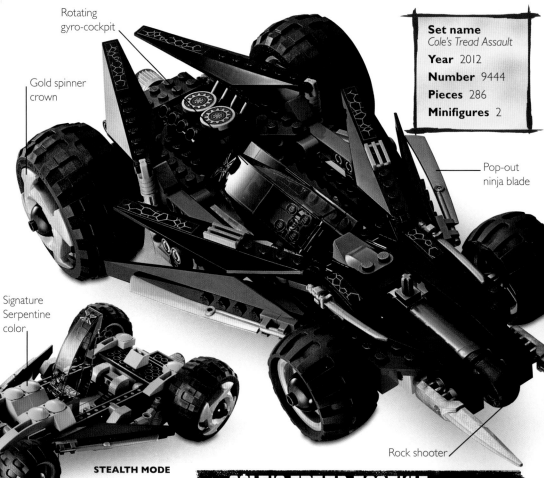

Rotating gyro-cockpit

Gold spinner crown

Set name
Cole's Tread Assault
Year 2012
Number 9444
Pieces 286
Minifigures 2

Pop-out ninja blade

▲ SPINJITZU COLE

When the ninja practice Spinjitzu, they spin rapidly to create an energy whirlwind around themselves. This tornado is made of small elemental particles. Since Cole is the Earth Ninja, his tornado is made of tiny earth particles, such as rocks and stones.

Signature Serpentine color

STEALTH MODE

Smaller, maneuverable front wheels

Rock shooter

▲ COLE'S TREAD ASSAULT

Cole is a master of tactics. He knows that to beat your enemy, you have to become your enemy. When Cole flips up his Tread Assault vehicle, its lime-green bricks fool his Serpentine foes into thinking it is one of their own green machines. This stealth mode function enables Cole to launch startling surprise attacks.

TRAINING COLE

Master Wu discovered his Earth Ninja when he saw Cole climb the highest mountain in Ninjago. Cole receives these black robes after the three other ninja have been found and the team is complete.

White face grille

KENDO COLE

Cole is always focused during ninja training and puts in hours of practice. When he trains in the ancient fighting style of kendo, Cole wears protective head and chest armor over his original ninja suit.

Bushy eyebrows

COLE DX

Cole likes people to think he is fearless, but there is one thing he can't hide: his fear of dragons! It is no mean feat for Cole to tame his Elemental Dragon and achieve DX (Dragon eXtreme) status.

COLE KIMONO

Cole receives these black-and-silver robes when Lloyd Garmadon is revealed to be the Ultimate Spinjitzu Master. Cole is a good teacher and helps Lloyd develop his ninja skills.

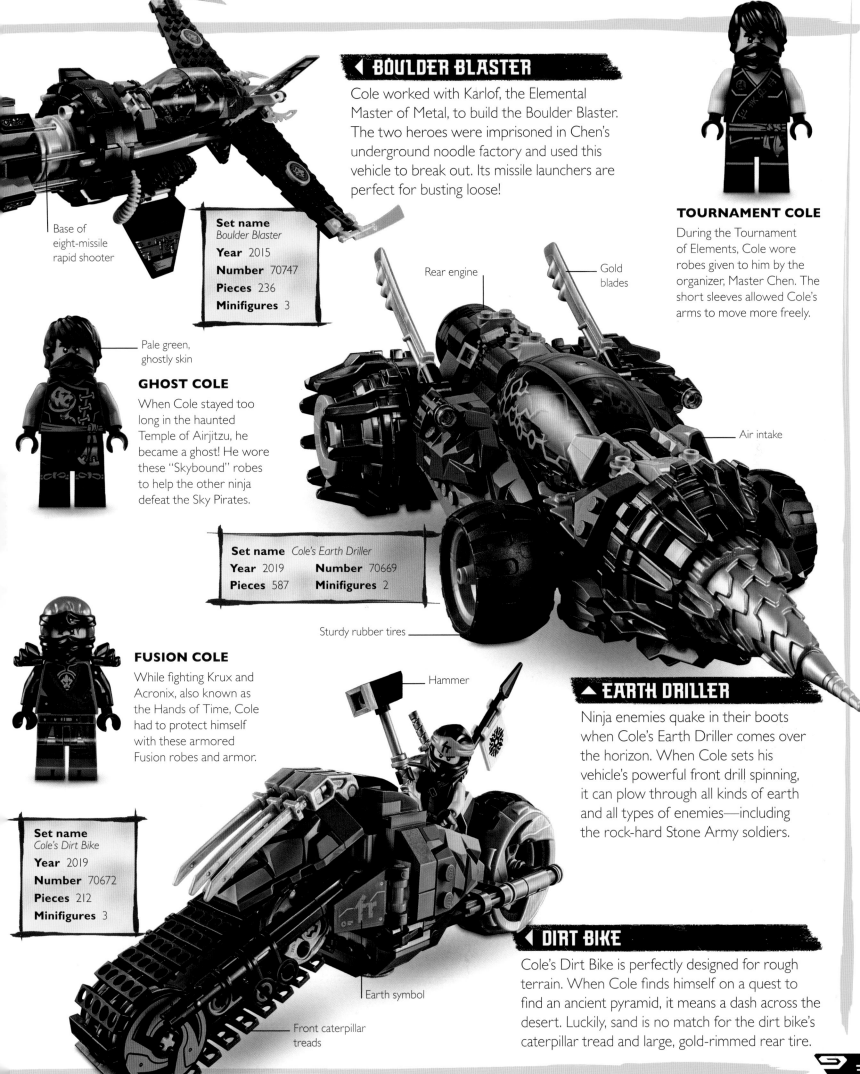

◀ BOULDER BLASTER

Cole worked with Karlof, the Elemental Master of Metal, to build the Boulder Blaster. The two heroes were imprisoned in Chen's underground noodle factory and used this vehicle to break out. Its missile launchers are perfect for busting loose!

Base of eight-missile rapid shooter

Set name *Boulder Blaster*
Year 2015
Number 70747
Pieces 236
Minifigures 3

TOURNAMENT COLE

During the Tournament of Elements, Cole wore robes given to him by the organizer, Master Chen. The short sleeves allowed Cole's arms to move more freely.

Pale green, ghostly skin

GHOST COLE

When Cole stayed too long in the haunted Temple of Airjitzu, he became a ghost! He wore these "Skybound" robes to help the other ninja defeat the Sky Pirates.

Rear engine

Gold blades

Air intake

Set name *Cole's Earth Driller*
Year 2019   **Number** 70669
Pieces 587   **Minifigures** 2

Sturdy rubber tires

FUSION COLE

While fighting Krux and Acronix, also known as the Hands of Time, Cole had to protect himself with these armored Fusion robes and armor.

Hammer

▲ EARTH DRILLER

Ninja enemies quake in their boots when Cole's Earth Driller comes over the horizon. When Cole sets his vehicle's powerful front drill spinning, it can plow through all kinds of earth and all types of enemies—including the rock-hard Stone Army soldiers.

Set name
Cole's Dirt Bike
Year 2019
Number 70672
Pieces 212
Minifigures 3

◀ DIRT BIKE

Cole's Dirt Bike is perfectly designed for rough terrain. When Cole finds himself on a quest to find an ancient pyramid, it means a dash across the desert. Luckily, sand is no match for the dirt bike's caterpillar tread and large, gold-rimmed rear tire.

Earth symbol

Front caterpillar treads

UNUSUAL ALLIES

The ninja have many friends who help them keep the peace in Ninjago. Some of these allies are quite unusual—they include a robot, a mysterious samurai, and an unexpectedly heroic thief! None of these allies are students of Master Wu, and none of them are Elemental Ninja—but they are all heroes in their own unique way!

P.I.X.A.L.

P.I.X.A.L. was originally tech genius Cyrus Borg's android assistant. This clever robot became the ninja's friend. She is especially close to Zane, who shares half his power core with her.

Circuits

Set name
Killow vs. Samurai X
Year 2018
Number 70642
Pieces 556
Minifigures 3

Hinged, retractable side blades

Golden Ninja sword blades

Samurai crest

P.I.X.A.L. SAMURAI X

Nya was the first to don the Samurai X armor. Later on, P.I.X.A.L. wore the armor and used it to help the ninja. P.I.X.A.L. personalized the armor in a new color—blue.

◀ SAMURAI X MECH

P.I.X.A.L. fights crime in her Samurai X armor. She has recolored and improved the mech that Nya wore. P.I.X.A.L.'s blue Samurai X Mech is a motion-controlled battle suit equipped with arm cannons and missiles. It is also able to fly.

Set name
Samurai VXL
Year 2017
Number 70625
Pieces 428
Minifigures 4

BRICK FACTS

Killow vs. Samurai X is the second NINJAGO set to feature a big fig (Killow). The first was Tiger Widow Island (set 70604), which included the big fig Dogshank.

Feet can smash through walls

Samurai X in cockpit

▶ SAMURAI VXL

When Nya became the Water Ninja, she gave the Samurai VXL car to the new Samurai X, who was secretly P.I.X.A.L. The vehicle was red when Nya owned it, but P.I.X.A.L. recolored it blue, just like her armor and mech!

Supercharged engine

DARETH

Dareth is a good-humored martial arts master. He is not one of Master Wu's students, but the ninja have accepted Dareth as one of their own and given him the title "Brown Ninja."

Trophy from Dareth's dojo

RONIN

Ronin is a thief, but he often helps Master Wu's team. Sometimes he can be greedy, and this brings him into conflict with the ninja. However, deep down, he has a good heart.

Twin shooters

Blasters are ready to shoot

▼ RONIN R.E.X.

Ronin's personal aircraft is called the Ronin R.E.X. It is programmed to respond when Ronin whistles, and is equipped with twin blasters. It is the perfect vehicle for a quick getaway!

Jet engine

Mini wing

Set name	Ronin R.E.X.	
Year	2015	Number 70735
Pieces	547	Minifigures 4

Gold shield

"Golden bow" launcher

Set name	Salvage M.E.C.	
Year	2016	Number 70592
Pieces	439	Minifigures 4

"Purple Ninja" costume

LIL' NELSON

Nelson was a young boy who was visited by the ninja in hospital. He helped them leave the hospital by holding off their fans. In gratitude, Lloyd named Nelson "Ninja for a Day."

◀ SALVAGE M.E.C.

The Salvage M.E.C. is an armored, high-powered mech created by Ronin. It is is armed with a bow-and-arrow-style launcher and an enormous net. Ronin uses the Salvage M.E.C. to help the ninja fight their enemies.

NINJA TRAINING

The ninja face all kinds of enemies who threaten the peace of Ninjago—from bony skeletons and slithering snakes to rock-hard Stone Soldiers and robotic Nindroids. The ninja must train hard to ensure they are ready to tackle anything. Master Wu ensures his ninja have the necessary training to help them do that.

The main training center for Master Wu's ninja team is the Spinjitzu Dojo. It's full of surprises to keep the ninja on their toes. Its entire length is filled with obstacles to tackle, including falling axes, exploding floorboards, a roaring fire pit, and fast-spinning katana swords.

Oriental curved roof

Flick-fire spear

Fortified wooden door

Falling ax

Plinth for Golden Weapons

Shuriken of Ice

Spinning katana

Set name	Ninja Training Outpost	
Year	2011	Number 2516
Pieces	45	Minifigures 1

Set name	Spinjitzu Dojo	
Year	2011	Number 2504
Pieces	373	Minifigures 3

Target

Scorpion

Dragon's head clasp

NINJA WEAPONS

At the dojo, monastery, and outpost, the ninja are trained to use a selection of impressive weapons.

Blossom on tree

NUNCHUCKS OF LIGHTNING

BOW AND ARROW

GOLD KATANAS

▲ NINJA TRAINING OUTPOST

This tower of weapons, located deep in the jungle, is the perfect place for some undisturbed weapons practice. The ninja have only a scorpion for company.

COLE IN TRAINING

Cole is focused on mastering the bow and arrow. He practices at the Ninja Training Outpost in the jungle. The golden dragon's-head clasp on his robes symbolizes his inner ferocity.

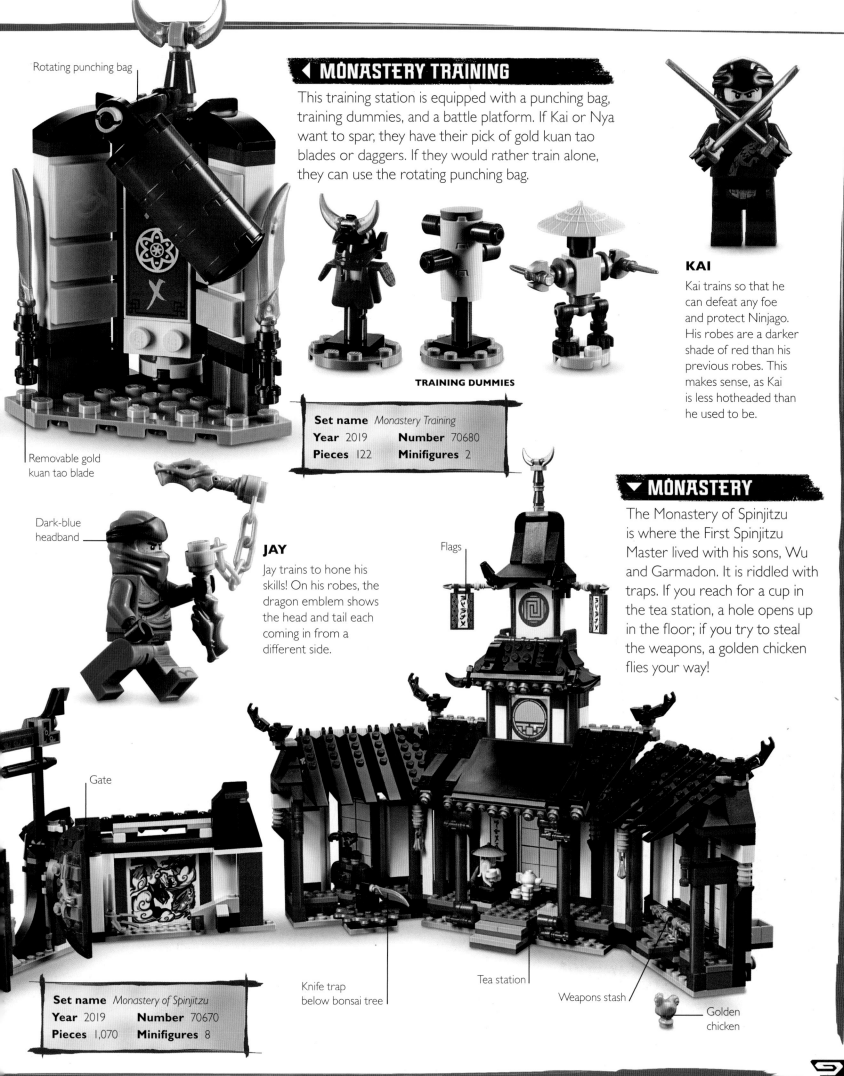

Rotating punching bag

Removable gold kuan tao blade

◀ MONASTERY TRAINING

This training station is equipped with a punching bag, training dummies, and a battle platform. If Kai or Nya want to spar, they have their pick of gold kuan tao blades or daggers. If they would rather train alone, they can use the rotating punching bag.

TRAINING DUMMIES

Set name	Monastery Training		
Year 2019		**Number** 70680	
Pieces 122		**Minifigures** 2	

KAI

Kai trains so that he can defeat any foe and protect Ninjago. His robes are a darker shade of red than his previous robes. This makes sense, as Kai is less hotheaded than he used to be.

Dark-blue headband

JAY

Jay trains to hone his skills! On his robes, the dragon emblem shows the head and tail each coming in from a different side.

Flags

▼ MONASTERY

The Monastery of Spinjitzu is where the First Spinjitzu Master lived with his sons, Wu and Garmadon. It is riddled with traps. If you reach for a cup in the tea station, a hole opens up in the floor; if you try to steal the weapons, a golden chicken flies your way!

Gate

Knife trap below bonsai tree

Tea station

Weapons stash

Golden chicken

Set name	Monastery of Spinjitzu	
Year 2019		**Number** 70670
Pieces 1,070		**Minifigures** 8

DRAGONS

These mystical creatures might look fierce, but only enemies of the ninja should fear them. Even the ninja were scared of the dragons before they realized that they share a common purpose: to protect Ninjago and the Golden Weapons. The dragons allied with the ninja, even serving as their transport for a time. For their part, the ninja helped dragon leader Firstbourne free her offspring from the barbaric Iron Baron and the Dragon Hunters.

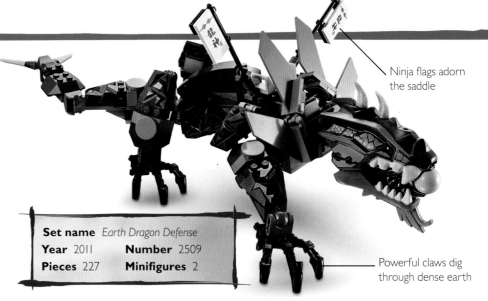

Ninja flags adorn the saddle

Set name	*Earth Dragon Defense*	
Year	2011	Number 2509
Pieces	227	Minifigures 2

Powerful claws dig through dense earth

▲ EARTH DRAGON

Guardian of the Scythe of Quakes, the Earth Dragon is the first Elemental Dragon the ninja encounter. Cole has a close bond with his dragon, whom he nicknames "Rocky" because of his rocklike hide. Rocky is the only Elemental Dragon who doesn't have wings.

Ice-tipped wing

◀ ICE DRAGON

The white-winged Ice Dragon can be hard to spot in the Frozen Wasteland, where Zane finds him guarding the Shurikens of Ice. Zane's dragon, whom he nicknames "Shard," chills his enemies by shooting freezing ice spheres from its mouth.

Set name	
Ice Dragon Attack	
Year	2011
Number	2260
Pieces	158
Minifigures	2

Strong reins

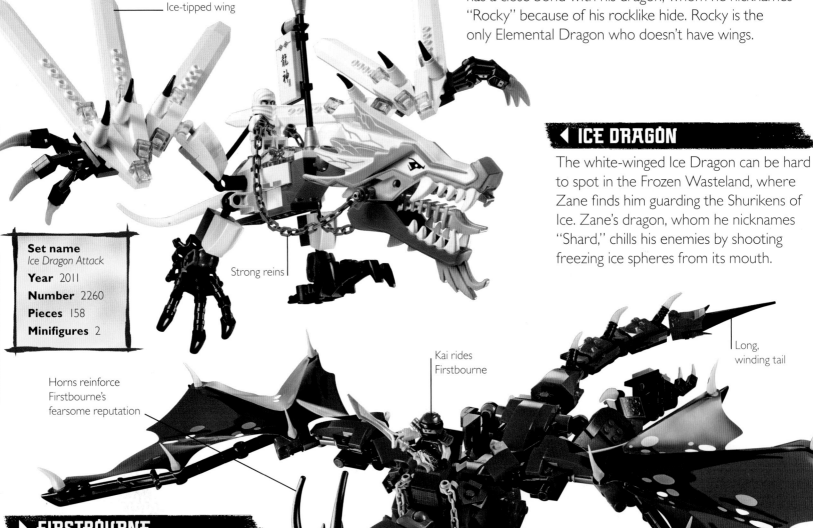

Kai rides Firstbourne

Long, winding tail

Horns reinforce Firstbourne's fearsome reputation

▶ FIRSTBOURNE

The legendary Mother of All Dragons, the Firstbourne is protective of her offspring, whom she freed from the Iron Baron and his Dragon Hunters. The Firstbourne befriended Master Wu and his ninja, letting them ride her and her children in a showdown against Lord Garmadon's forces.

Claws can repel Dragon Hunters

Set name	*Firstbourne*	
Year	2018	Number 70653
Pieces	882	Minifigures 6

▶ GREEN NRG DRAGON

Also known as the Energy Dragon, the Green Dragon is not a physical creature, but rather a reflection of Lloyd's emotions. Whenever Lloyd gives in to fear, the dragon disappears. The amount of concentration needed to maintain its existence means that the dragon can only fly short distances.

Lloyd is in the saddle

Huge, batlike wings

Talons

Set name *Green NRG Dragon*
Year 2016
Number 70593
Pieces 567
Minifigures 5

One of four dragon heads

The Green Ninja at the reins

Wings flare out when in flight

◀ ULTRA DRAGON

The four Elemental Dragons morph into one to become the Ultra Dragon. It can be controlled only by the most powerful ninja. When Lloyd becomes the Green Ninja, he takes control of the Ultra Dragon to battle an enormous snake called the Great Devourer.

Clawlike talons

Set name *Ultra Dragon (Legacy)*
Year 2019   **Number** 70679
Pieces 951   **Minifigures** 6

Armrests on the saddle

Fearsome tail sweeps away enemies

▶ STORMBRINGER

Stormbringer normally lives in the Realm of Dragons and Oni, but crosses into Ninjago through a portal. This Lightning Dragon briefly teams up with Jay, the Lightning Ninja, to battle the Sons of Garmadon. After defeating the villains, Stormbringer returns to its realm.

Dragon Hunter Daddy No Legs reins in Stormbringer

Set name *Stormbringer*
Year 2018
Number 70652
Pieces 493
Minifigures 4

Creature's mouth spits lightning bolts

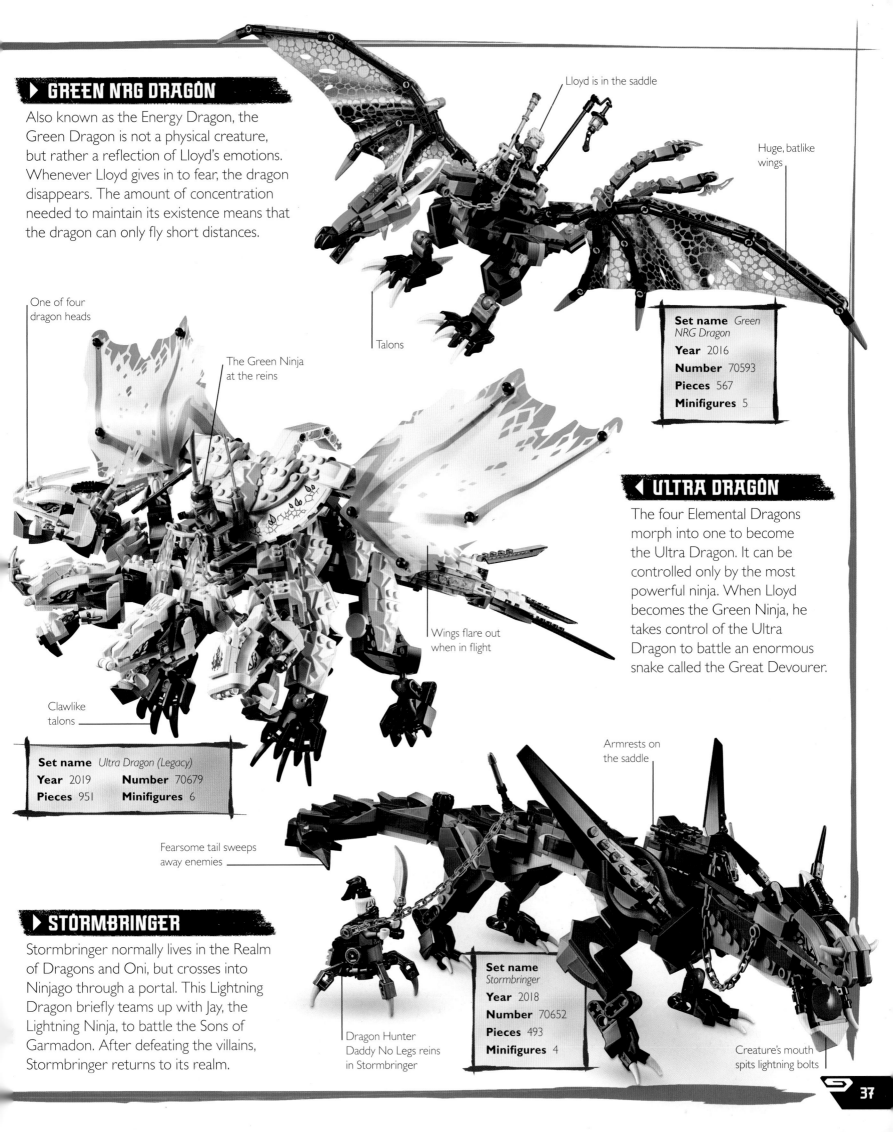

TEMPLES

Many of the ninja's most momentous journeys and adventures have involved temples of various kinds. Usually, a temple is a place of solitude, where the ninja train and meditate. Sometimes, it is a headquarters where the ninja make their plans. Occasionally, a temple is the battleground for an epic clash with a formidable opponent. However, as long as the ninja have each other, no foe is unstoppable!

Set name	*Temple of Light*	
Year 2013	**Number**	70505
Pieces 565	**Minifigures**	5

▶ TEMPLE OF LIGHT

This ninja temple lies atop a large mountain on the Island of Darkness. It is home to the Elemental Blades, which can enhance the ninja's elemental powers. Wu and the ninja are pursued by Stone Soldiers as they reach the temple—but if any of them get close to the Elemental Blades, Wu can release a secret trap door to eject the soldiers.

Golden
Dragon flag

Chamber for
the Elemental
Blades

Stone Army
Swordsman

Weapons
rack

Murals depicting
ancient ninja
masters

Trap door
rack

Front walls split apart if
the Dragon Sword of
Fire is tampered with

Dragon-printed
panels

Dragon
Sword
of Fire

Mini-dragon statue

◀ FIRE TEMPLE

This flaming ninja temple is located inside an active volcano. Master Wu hid the Dragon Sword of Fire there to keep it from his wayward brother. If Lord Garmadon or any of his henchmen attempt to steal the Sword, the Fire Temple splits open to reveal the wrath of the mighty Fire Dragon that guards the weapon.

Set name	
Fire Temple	
Year	2011
Number	2507
Pieces	1,174
Minifigures	7

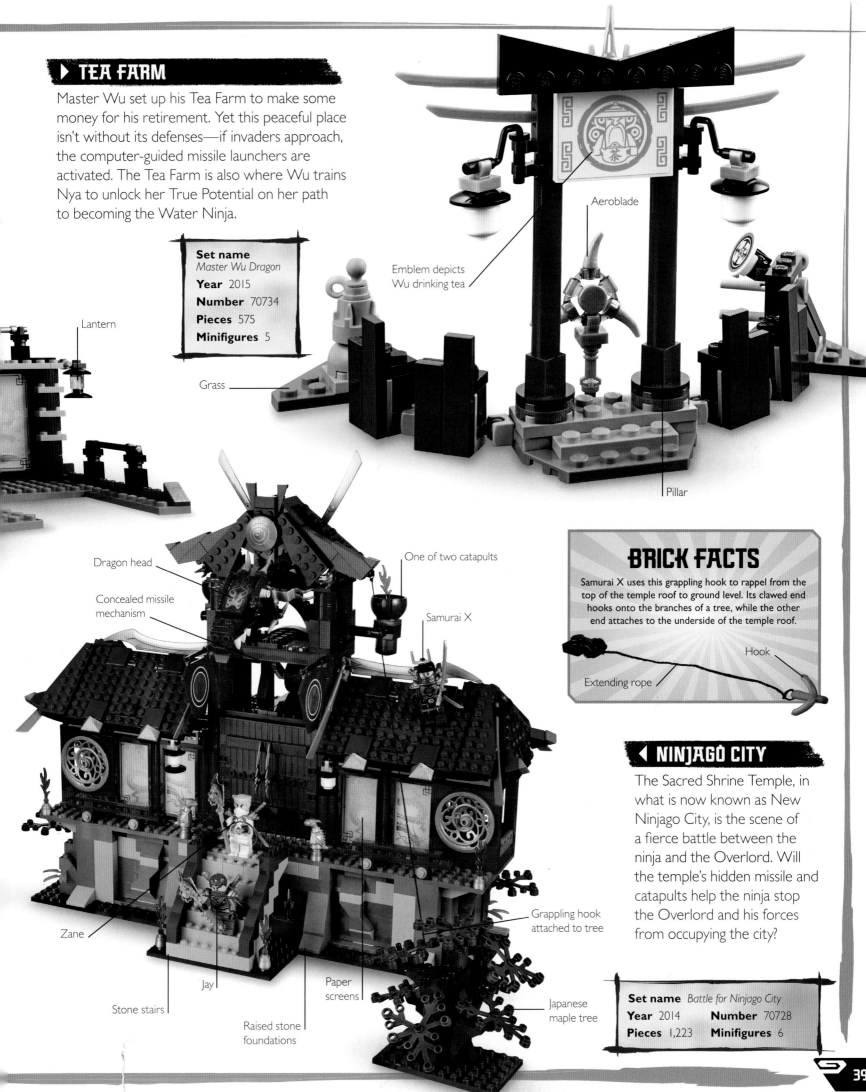

▶ TEA FARM

Master Wu set up his Tea Farm to make some money for his retirement. Yet this peaceful place isn't without its defenses—if invaders approach, the computer-guided missile launchers are activated. The Tea Farm is also where Wu trains Nya to unlock her True Potential on her path to becoming the Water Ninja.

Set name
Master Wu Dragon
Year 2015
Number 70734
Pieces 575
Minifigures 5

Lantern

Grass

Aeroblade

Emblem depicts
Wu drinking tea

Pillar

Dragon head

Concealed missile
mechanism

One of two catapults

Samurai X

Zane

Jay

Stone stairs

Raised stone
foundations

Paper
screens

Grappling hook
attached to tree

Japanese
maple tree

BRICK FACTS

Samurai X uses this grappling hook to rappel from the top of the temple roof to ground level. Its clawed end hooks onto the branches of a tree, while the other end attaches to the underside of the temple roof.

Hook

Extending rope

◀ NINJAGO CITY

The Sacred Shrine Temple, in what is now known as New Ninjago City, is the scene of a fierce battle between the ninja and the Overlord. Will the temple's hidden missile and catapults help the ninja stop the Overlord and his forces from occupying the city?

Set name *Battle for Ninjago City*
Year 2014   **Number** 70728
Pieces 1,223   **Minifigures** 6

TEMPLE OF AIRJITZU

The Temple of Airjitzu is where Master Wu and his ninja warriors train and relax. For some time, it was haunted by the ghost of Master Yang. He was the creator of Airjitzu, a martial art that allows someone to temporarily fly. When he stopped haunting the temple, it was restored and the ninja began using it as their base. Yang's spirit still occupies the temple, but the ghost exists in harmony alongside the ninja.

Set name
Temple of Airjitzu
Year 2015
Number 70751
Pieces 2,028
Minifigures 13

▶ TERRIFIC TEMPLE

With its striking red walls, elegantly decorated windows, and beautiful sliding doors, the temple is a true architectural marvel. It is the perfect ninja home, serving many different roles—Master Wu uses it to meditate, Misako uses it to paint, and the ninja use it to improve their skills.

Windows have hand-painted decorations

Nya takes photos of scenery

MISAKO

Misako is an archaeologist and also a Spinjitzu Master. She goes on adventures with her son, Lloyd, and was Lord Garmadon's wife before he became villainous.

Neckerchief is green, in honor of Lloyd

CLAIRE

Claire is a tourist visiting the Temple of Airjitzu. She is hired by the ninja to help clean and repair the temple. Claire is the daughter of Jesper.

JESPER

Jesper is Claire's father. He is passionate about fishing. Unlike his brave daughter, he is afraid to approach the Temple of Airjitzu because it used to be haunted.

Mailbag full of letters

POSTMAN

The postman is a mail courier in Ninjago. Sometimes he goes to great lengths to deliver the mail to the ninja.

Lloyd surveys the area

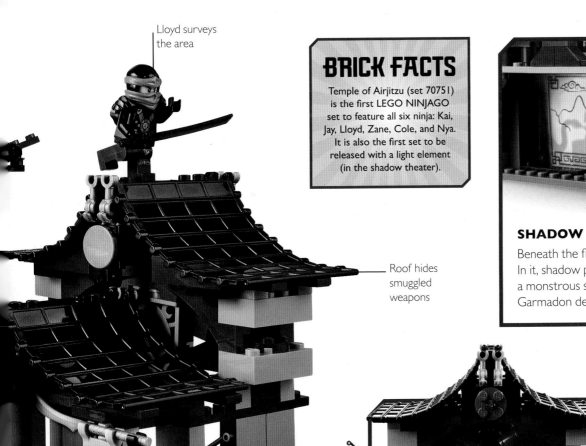

Roof hides smuggled weapons

BRICK FACTS

Temple of Airjitzu (set 70751) is the first LEGO NINJAGO set to feature all six ninja: Kai, Jay, Lloyd, Zane, Cole, and Nya. It is also the first set to be released with a light element (in the shadow theater).

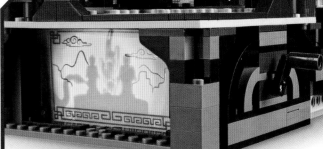

SHADOW THEATER

Beneath the first floor of the temple is a shadow theater. In it, shadow puppets tell the story of the Great Devourer, a monstrous serpent that wreaked havoc until Lord Garmadon destroyed it.

SMUGGLERS' MARKET

Next to the temple is the Smugglers' Market, where smuggled weapons are stashed inside the roof. Shop at any of the vendors' stalls and you'll see they're selling everything from baguettes to fish to Ninjago trading cards! Under the roof, a pulley is used to transport goods.

NINJA VEHICLES

Sometimes Master Wu and his team of young warriors need to get somewhere in super-quick time. That's where their fantastic ninja vehicles come in. The ninja use these vehicles to go where they're needed. These high-tech trucks, planes, boats, and airships help our heroes fight villainous forces in Ninjago, as well as in other realms.

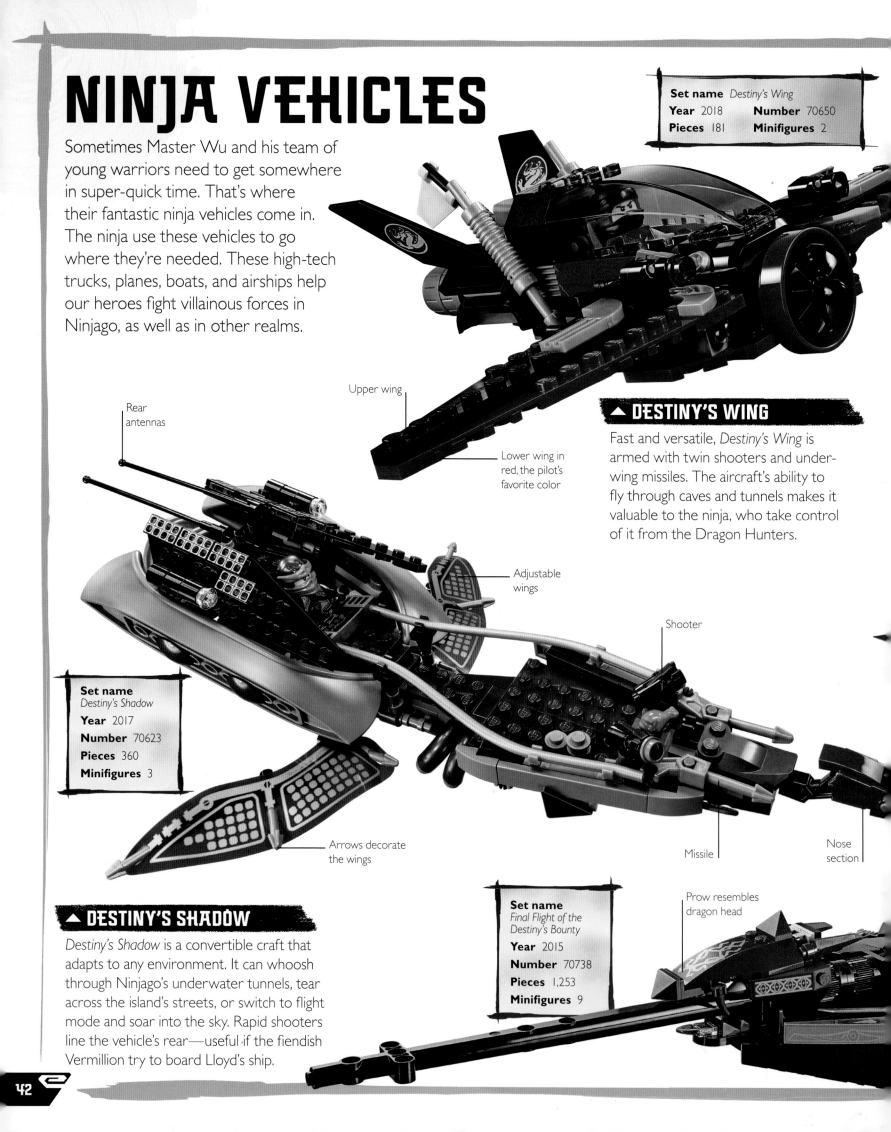

Set name	*Destiny's Wing*	
Year 2018	**Number**	70650
Pieces 181	**Minifigures**	2

Upper wing

Rear antennas

Lower wing in red, the pilot's favorite color

▲ DESTINY'S WING

Fast and versatile, *Destiny's Wing* is armed with twin shooters and under-wing missiles. The aircraft's ability to fly through caves and tunnels makes it valuable to the ninja, who take control of it from the Dragon Hunters.

Adjustable wings

Shooter

Set name		
Destiny's Shadow		
Year 2017		
Number 70623		
Pieces 360		
Minifigures 3		

Arrows decorate the wings

Missile

Nose section

▲ DESTINY'S SHADOW

Destiny's Shadow is a convertible craft that adapts to any environment. It can whoosh through Ninjago's underwater tunnels, tear across the island's streets, or switch to flight mode and soar into the sky. Rapid shooters line the vehicle's rear—useful if the fiendish Vermillion try to board Lloyd's ship.

Set name		
Final Flight of the Destiny's Bounty		
Year 2015		
Number 70738		
Pieces 1,253		
Minifigures 9		

Prow resembles dragon head

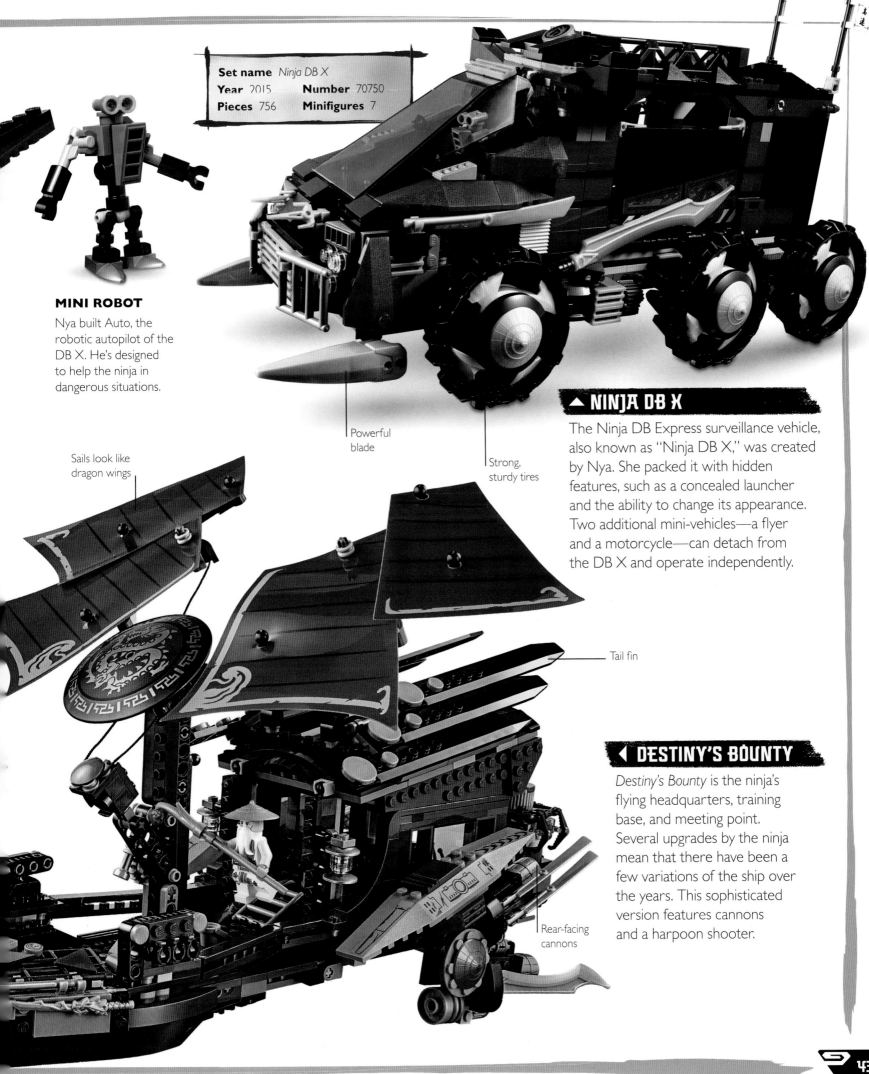

Set name	*Ninja DB X*		
Year	2015	**Number**	70750
Pieces	756	**Minifigures**	7

MINI ROBOT

Nya built Auto, the robotic autopilot of the DB X. He's designed to help the ninja in dangerous situations.

Sails look like dragon wings

Powerful blade

Strong, sturdy tires

▲ NINJA DB X

The Ninja DB Express surveillance vehicle, also known as "Ninja DB X," was created by Nya. She packed it with hidden features, such as a concealed launcher and the ability to change its appearance. Two additional mini-vehicles—a flyer and a motorcycle—can detach from the DB X and operate independently.

Tail fin

◀ DESTINY'S BOUNTY

Destiny's Bounty is the ninja's flying headquarters, training base, and meeting point. Several upgrades by the ninja mean that there have been a few variations of the ship over the years. This sophisticated version features cannons and a harpoon shooter.

Rear-facing cannons

ULTRA STEALTH RAIDER

The Ultra Stealth Raider was originally designed for use by the Sky Pirates before being captured by the ninja. When it's not one giant vehicle, it splits into four mini-vehicles: a helijet, a huge bike, and two tread bikes. Yet just as the ninja do their best work as a team, this vehicle is more powerful when its modules come together to form one unstoppable machine.

▼ HIGH-TECH TANK

When villains see the Ultra Stealth Raider coming over the horizon, they had better take cover! The ninja use this vehicle when they're facing off against an intimidating foe, like the ghostly Master Yang. Good thing this high-tech tank brims with features and detachable golden weapons.

JAY'S TREAD BIKE

When Jay disengages his tread bike from the Ultra Stealth Raider, his enemies had better move fast! This super-speedy vehicle has a rear wheel for extra maneuverability. As well as being nimble, it's also able to wipe out villains with a flick-fire missile on the left-hand side.

Streamlined cockpit

BIG BIKE

Once the tread bikes and the helijet detach from the vehicle, Cole can steady his big bike using its convertible wheel. The bike can now bank, tilt, and make easy turns on any surface.

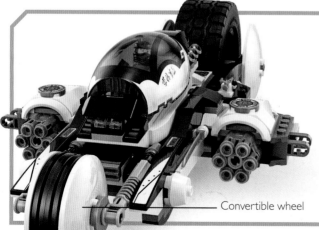

Convertible wheel

BRICK FACTS

Ultra Stealth Raider (set 70595) is only the second NINJAGO set to come with just the four original ninja (Cole, Kai, Jay, and Zane). The first was this set's predecessor, Ultra Sonic Raider (set 9449).

HELIJET

Zane is a master of technology, so he appreciates a cutting-edge craft like the helijet. When its foldout wings have extended, it cuts through the air like a ninja blade! This sleek vehicle is stocked with two gold shuriken and a prison cell under the rear section that can hold a captured rogue.

Blade wing

Flight deck

Rapid shooter

Extra-wide rear wheel

Set name
Ultra Stealth Raider
Year 2016
Number 70595
Pieces 1,093
Minifigures 7

KAI'S TREAD BIKE

Kai burns across the desert in his own tread bike. It's exactly the same as Jay's vehicle, except for the different color scheme—red, to reflect Kai's colors.

Flick-fire missile

Sharp front blades

Stabilizing tread

MECHS

These enormous fighting machines are built for a ninja in need of some additional battle power. Kai, Cole, Lloyd Garmadon (as the Golden Ninja), and even the First Spinjitzu Master have all commanded the cockpits of robotic mechs. They use them to fight villains in Ninjago and gain the advantage in battle.

Katana sword out of enemies' reach

▶ KAI'S FIRE MECH

Kai hops into the cockpit of this mech when he needs to turn up the heat in battle against the Stone Army. With a huge cannon on one arm and a robotic hand grasping the Dragon Sword of Fire in the other, the Fire Mech has the power to turn Kai's stone enemies to dust.

Set name *Kai's Fire Mech*
Year 2013   **Number** 70500
Pieces 102   **Minifigures** 2

Control column

Towering legs have the power to scale mountains

Impenetrable armor

Grasping golden digits

Metal harness holds Cole in place

Blaster cannon

Golden Ninja sword

Set name
Thunder Raider
Year 2014
Number 70723
Pieces 334
Minifigures 3

Wide feet can flatten Nindroids

◀ COLE'S MECH

Cole's almighty Earth Mech is built to overwhelm his Nindroid enemies, and it is a mech with an extraordinary advantage. When Cole teams up with the Lightning Ninja, Jay, Cole's mech can attach to the back of Jay's lightning off-roader to form a mighty Thunder Raider vehicle.

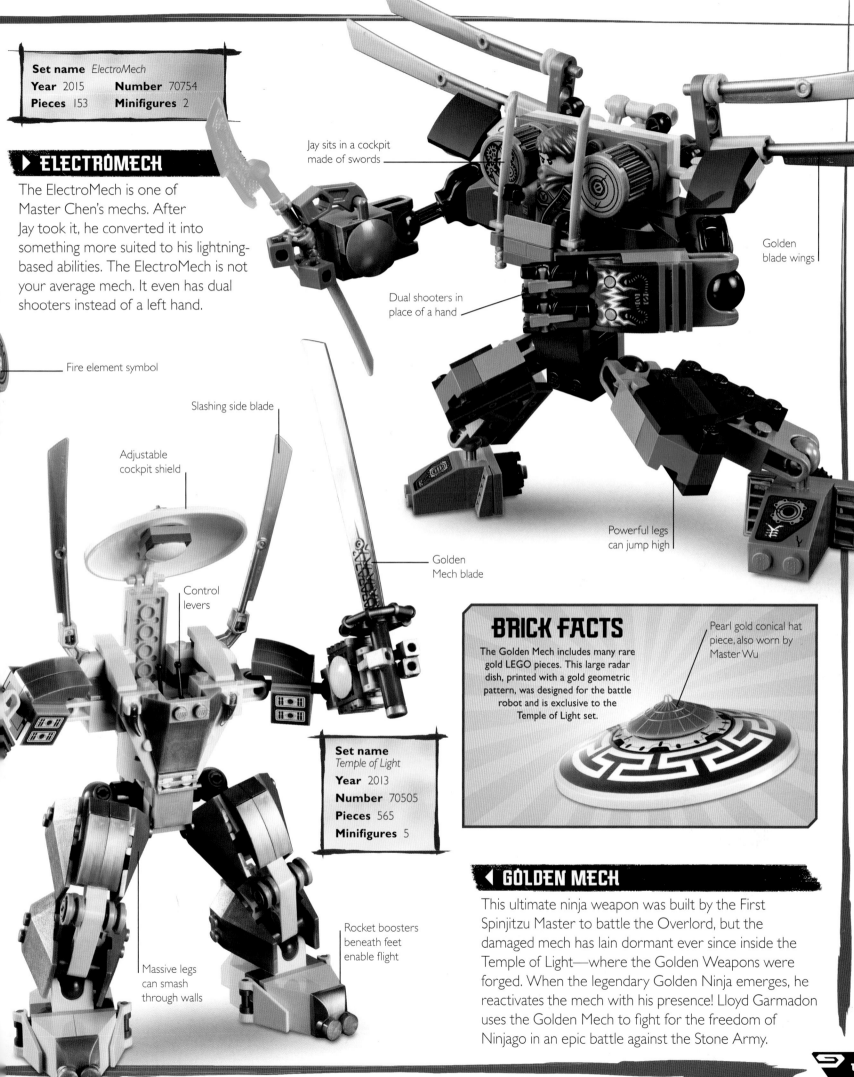

Set name *ElectroMech*
Year 2015   **Number** 70754
Pieces 153   **Minifigures** 2

▶ ELECTROMECH

The ElectroMech is one of Master Chen's mechs. After Jay took it, he converted it into something more suited to his lightning-based abilities. The ElectroMech is not your average mech. It even has dual shooters instead of a left hand.

Jay sits in a cockpit made of swords

Golden blade wings

Fire element symbol

Dual shooters in place of a hand

Slashing side blade

Adjustable cockpit shield

Golden Mech blade

Control levers

Powerful legs can jump high

Set name *Temple of Light*
Year 2013
Number 70505
Pieces 565
Minifigures 5

BRICK FACTS

The Golden Mech includes many rare gold LEGO pieces. This large radar dish, printed with a gold geometric pattern, was designed for the battle robot and is exclusive to the Temple of Light set.

Pearl gold conical hat piece, also worn by Master Wu

Massive legs can smash through walls

Rocket boosters beneath feet enable flight

◀ GOLDEN MECH

This ultimate ninja weapon was built by the First Spinjitzu Master to battle the Overlord, but the damaged mech has lain dormant ever since inside the Temple of Light—where the Golden Weapons were forged. When the legendary Golden Ninja emerges, he reactivates the mech with his presence! Lloyd Garmadon uses the Golden Mech to fight for the freedom of Ninjago in an epic battle against the Stone Army.

CHAPTER 2:
FOES

LORD GARMADON

Lord Garmadon, the brother of Master Wu and father of Lloyd Garmadon, wasn't born bad. He was infected when he was bitten by a serpent called the Great Devourer. From then on, he is transformed into a venomous villain with an all-consuming desire to destroy Ninjago.

Underworld helmet

Visible ribs

▲ LORD GARMADON

When Garmadon became a villain, he dueled with his brother, Wu. Wu was victorious and banished Garmadon to the Underworld. Garmadon's skin turned completely black, his bones and teeth glowed white, and his eyes glowed red—his transformation was complete.

Set name	Garmadon's Dark Fortress		
Year	2011	Number	2505
Pieces	518	Minifigures	6

Missile launcher

Spider attachment

Spinning watchtower

Skulkins symbol

Prison cell

Tusk-flanked drawbridge

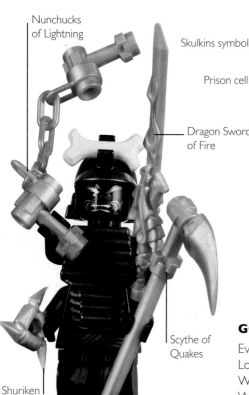

Nunchucks of Lightning

Dragon Sword of Fire

Scythe of Quakes

Shuriken of Ice

GOLDEN WEAPONS OF SPINJITZU

Ever since his evil transformation, it has been Lord Garmadon's goal to seize the Golden Weapons of Spinjitzu from his brother, Wu. With four arms and enhanced powers, he now has the rare ability to wield all four weapons at once—a colossal feat. Lord Garmadon unites the four Golden Weapons in the Epic Dragon Battle.

▲ DARK FORTRESS

When Lord Garmadon arrives in the Underworld, he claims the crown of King of the Underworld, takes control of the Skulkins, and moves into this fearsome fortress. While his skeletal minions keep a constant watch for intruders from the fortified towers, Garmadon surveys his new dark domain from his flying throne.

Full head
of gray hair

Ninja
robes

Green sash

◢ MASTER GARMADON

Is this really Lord Garmadon? He
has renounced his villainous past
and returned to his human form.
Now an old man, with gray hair
and a wrinkled face, Master
Garmadon acts as a mentor to
his beloved son, Lloyd, and the
other ninja. He even sacrifices
his life to save Ninjago.

▼ PROTO SAM-X

Now a friend of the ninja, Garmadon
helps his son, Lloyd, battle against the
MechDragon. Here, Garmadon drives
the Proto Sam-X. It's equipped with
a rotating harpoon missile, two laser
cannons, and hidden missile launchers.

Harpoon

Missile
launcher

Garmadon in
the cockpit

Concealed
flick-fire missile

Katanas act as
front bumper

Set name
*Nindroid
MechDragon*

Year 2014

Number 70725

Pieces 691

Minifigures 5

Commanding staff

Stone Army horn

Yellow glint in eye

Purple energy oozes
out of cracked armor

HELMET OF
SHADOWS

Lord Garmadon may have a
new helmet, but he is still up
to his old tricks. The Helmet
of Shadows gives Garmadon
control over the Stone Army
and starts the Celestial
Clock, which counts down to
the prophesized final battle
for Ninjago.

▶ RESURRECTED
GARMADON

When Princess Harumi unites
all three Oni Masks, Lord
Garmadon is brought back to life.
He is now more powerful than
ever. He masters the powers of
Destruction and Creation and
uses them to battle the ninja.

THE SKULKINS

The Skulkins are from the Underworld—a shadowy realm where the dead of Ninjago come back to life. The bony battalion is working for Lord Garmadon, who has made himself King of the Underworld. Their master wants to find the Golden Weapons and use their combined power to control Ninjago. All Skulkins are prepared to go to any lengths—and take down any ninja—to make that happen.

Metal helmet

Skulkin symbol

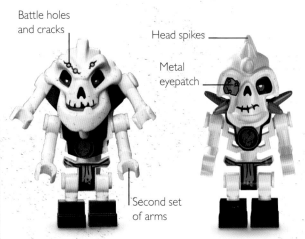

Battle holes and cracks

Head spikes

Metal eyepatch

Second set of arms

SAMUKAI

This four-armed Skulkin ruled the Underworld before Lord Garmadon arrived. Now Garmadon's deputy, Samukai has a mouth that opens—this helps him bark orders to his troops!

NUCKAL

Fighting is Nuckal's idea of fun, but this hotheaded general gets into scrapes too often. He lost an eye in battle and replaced it with a bolted-on eyepatch.

▶ KRUNCHA

Kruncha takes his role very seriously. He is the only Skulkin to always wear his metal helmet, which is attached to his skull head piece. Kruncha's hard work for the Skulkins eventually pays off—he becomes their leader when his boss, Samukai, is defeated in battle.

▶ NUCKAL'S ATV

This bad-boy vehicle has a four-wheeled suspension system that can tear up any terrain. Below its scary, skull-shaped hood is a hidden missile launcher.

Exhaust flame

Tusks protect the rear

Throttle lever

Spiked bone ax

READY FOR BATTLE

When Nuckal appears in his ATV and at the Spinjitzu Dojo, he has movable hand clips so he can wield a weapon more effectively.

Set name		
Nuckal's ATV		
Year 2011		
Number 2518		
Pieces 174		
Minifigures 2		

▼ SKULL TRUCK

The Skull Truck's array of weapons is the stuff of ninja nightmares. At the front, a ninja can be held captive inside the jaws of the skull bumper, which snap as the truck's front suspension bounces. At its rear are a bone fist launcher and two bone-barred ninja prison pods.

Bone fist fired from truck

Prison pod

Engine

Exhaust flames

BRICK FACTS
The Skull Truck (set 2506) has a suspension system made from LEGO® Technic bricks, beams, pins, and shock absorbers, which give it additional movement capabilities.

Set name
Skull Truck
Year 2011
Number 2506
Pieces 515
Minifigures 4

Spiked wheel hub

Rubber tire

Heavily grooved tires

KRAZI

Krazi is as insane as his name suggests. The wild and unpredictable skeleton wears crazy-looking clown makeup that serves as a warning to his enemies. He is one frightening foe!

WYPLASH

Wyplash is a suspicious general who likes to secretly keep an eye on his enemies from under his conical hat. After clashing with the ninja, Wyplash is sent to Kryptarium Prison.

KRAZI WITH JESTER'S HAT

Krazi has been known to wear just a jester's hat and no Skulkin armor. He may look like a fool, but be warned—Krazi's fighting skills are no joke!

WEAPONS WIELDER

Most of the time, Wyplash has vertical hands, so he can point his weaponry right at his enemies. Occasionally, Wyplash's hands are horizontal, letting his weapon whack foes from the side as he whirls around.

SKULKIN SOLDIERS

Skulkin generals may ride in the mightiest Skulkin vehicles, but even the lower-ranking warriors command some scary-looking rides. These soldiers all have the same objective: to annoy and destroy the ninja.

Set name	Lightning Dragon Battle	
Year	2011	Number 2521
Pieces	645	Minifigures 4

Skeleton-head missile

Rotor

▶ SKULL COPTER

The Skulkins love to build vehicles in its own image. This Skull Copter is a flying skull, with snapping jaws and a cockpit (with room for one pilot) beneath the forehead. Its skeleton-head missiles on either side of the skull can flick-fire enemies from great heights.

Tail rotor blade

Grab hook lowers to capture enemies

Printed skull symbol

Bone landing skids

Rear engine

Roaring flames

Rear wheels

Frakjaw at the controls

Set name	
Turbo Shredder	
Year	2011
Number	2263
Pieces	298
Minifigures	3

AVIATOR FRAKJAW

Frakjaw wears a pilot hat and goggles to fly the Skull Copter. He also carries a whipping mace ball—his favorite weapon.

Skull head poised to swallow a ninja

Bone-encased cockpit

▶ TURBO SHREDDER

When its front treads roll, the Turbo Shredder can swallow a ninja whole. The movement of the vehicle's rubber treads makes the fanged skull at the front rise up above a standing warrior, then down to capture him.

FRAKJAW

If Frakjaw doesn't take down enemies with Skulkin vehicles, he may talk them to death instead. The chatty Skeleton wears a straw hat to pilot the Turbo Shredder.

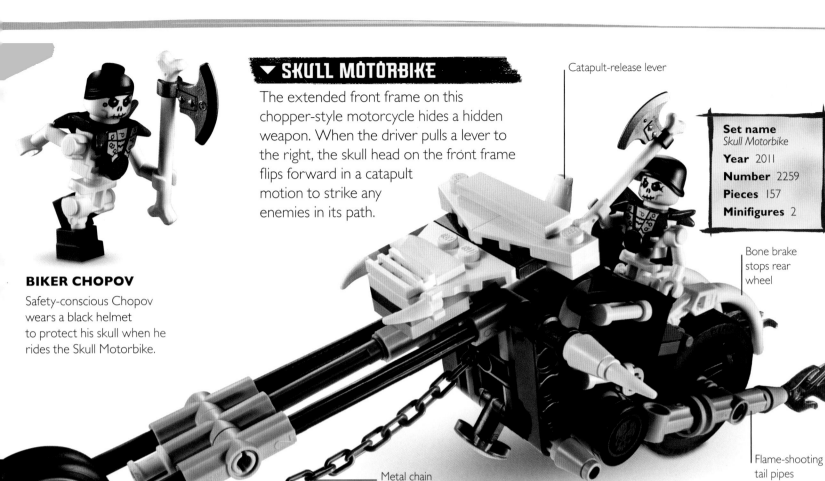

▼ SKULL MOTORBIKE

The extended front frame on this chopper-style motorcycle hides a hidden weapon. When the driver pulls a lever to the right, the skull head on the front frame flips forward in a catapult motion to strike any enemies in its path.

Catapult-release lever

BIKER CHOPOV

Safety-conscious Chopov wears a black helmet to protect his skull when he rides the Skull Motorbike.

Bone brake stops rear wheel

Metal chain

Flame-shooting tail pipes

Set name	
Skull Motorbike	
Year	2011
Number	2259
Pieces	157
Minifigures	2

BONEZAI UNARMED

Bonezai may seem underdressed, but he's actually rarely seen in his armor. Most of the time he appears without any protective clothing.

Armor shows rank of soldier

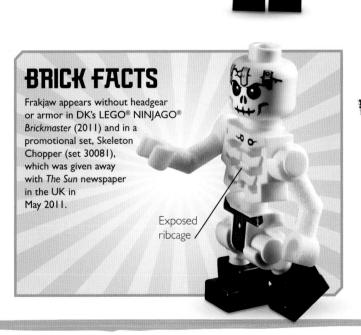

BRICK FACTS

Frakjaw appears without headgear or armor in DK's LEGO® NINJAGO® *Brickmaster* (2011) and in a promotional set, Skeleton Chopper (set 30081), which was given away with *The Sun* newspaper in the UK in May 2011.

Exposed ribcage

▲ BONEZAI

Bonezai's strange red eyes may give him a dim-witted look, but this Skulkin is clever. As head designer of the Skulkin vehicles, Bonezai's job is to build the fastest wheels possible, though it doesn't always go to plan!

▲ CHOPOV

As chief mechanic of the Skulkins, Chopov is responsible for making sure that the Skulkins' fleet of vehicles run like clockwork. Chopov usually wears dark-gray body armor. However, he is sometimes seen in Frakjaw's red Skeleton of Fire armor.

THE SERPENTINE

This snake race once ruled Ninjago. The Serpentine are made up of five different tribes, each with unique abilities. The tribes warred for centuries, until the people of Ninjago rose up against their rule and locked them away in five separate tombs. Centuries later, they are back—and ready to wage war on Ninjago.

FLYING VEHICLE

Firing engines

LAND VEHICLE

Set name
Ultra Sonic Raider
Year 2012
Number 9449
Pieces 622
Minifigures 6

▲ ULTRA SONIC RAIDER

When the Great Devourer destroys *Destiny's Bounty*, the ninja fuse their elemental powers together to build the Ultra Sonic Raider. It can launch a two-pronged attack on their fork-tongued enemies, by land and by air.

TRAP JAW

There is a minifigure-sized space inside the Great Devourer's mouth. When the top jaw snaps shut, the minifigure is trapped inside.

Jay

PYTHOR

Pythor P. Chumsworth is the last surviving member of his tribe, the Anacondrai. He was found by Lloyd in the Anacondrai tomb, and the two went on to become friends.

WHITE PYTHOR

When Pythor tried to control the Great Devourer, he was eaten by the frightening beast. As a result, Pythor spent time in the Great Devourer's stomach. The experience turned his skin white.

Menacing fangs

White robes

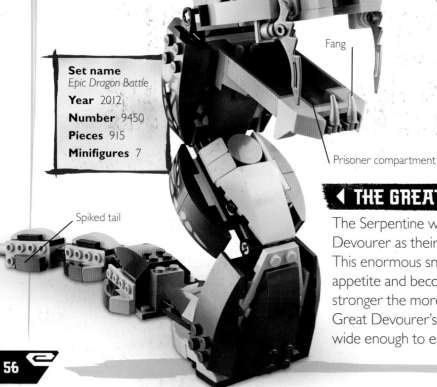

Evil eyes

Fang

Set name
Epic Dragon Battle
Year 2012
Number 9450
Pieces 915
Minifigures 7

Spiked tail

Prisoner compartment

▶ SNAKE PRISON

When Master Wu is taken by the Great Devourer, he is held in this impenetrable snake prison. He has scratched off his number of days in captivity on one of the prison's walls.

◀ THE GREAT DEVOURER

The Serpentine worship the Great Devourer as their god and ruler. This enormous snake has a huge appetite and becomes larger and stronger the more it consumes. The Great Devourer's jaws open up wide enough to eat a ninja whole.

Viper fountain

Scimitar sword

Snake heads dripping with venom

Deadly spider

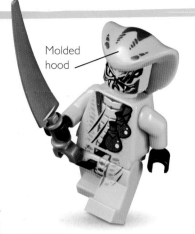

Molded hood

LASHA

The Venomari tribe have four yellow eyes, except for three-eyed scout Lasha, who lost one in battle. His head features two scars where his eye once was.

There's no mistaking whose toxic green ride this is—it looks a lot like him! Lasha can lash out at his enemies with his Bite Cycle's whipping tail, which moves up and down and side to side.

Lasha, blending in

Snake head hood

Side missile

Toxic flame

Set name *Lasha's Bite Cycle*
Year 2012   **Number** 9447
Pieces 250   **Minifigures** 2

◄ GENERAL ACIDICUS

Like all Serpentine leaders, General Acidicus has a long, snaking tail instead of the humanoid legs of his inferiors. The Venomari leader is the brains of the tribe, though they are not known for their intelligence!

LIZARU

Venomari warrior Lizaru is Acidicus's deputy. He likes hunting and eating large prey, after which he can go off to enjoy another of his favorite pastimes—sleeping!

Set name *Venomari Shrine*
Year 2012   **Number** 9440
Pieces 86   **Minifigures** 1

Mini-snake, ready to be fired

Mini-snake launch pad

SPITTA

Venomari soldier Spitta carries two red vials of venom into battle so he never runs out—a tactic masterminded by his leader, Acidicus.

► VENOMARI SHRINE

Inside this shrine, surrounded by toxic snake slime, is the Venomari snake staff, which contains precious antivenom. Be warned—any ninja who tries to take the staff may suffer a surprise mini-snake attack.

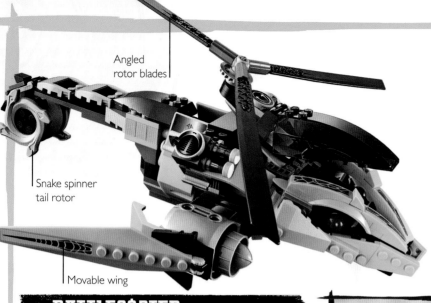

Angled rotor blades

Snake spinner tail rotor

Movable wing

SERPENTINE TRIBES

A bite from a member of the Fangpyre tribe turns creatures into snake people, while the Constrictai's powerful grip makes them the strongest of the Serpentines. The Hypnobrai's powers lie in their red, swirling eyes—which hypnotize their victims!

▲ RATTLECOPTER

The Rattlecopter is a fast and effective Fangpyre aircraft. The one-man cockpit, manned by Fang-Suei, is built into its snake-head fuselage. Its bomb-drop feature rains venomous mini-snakes on the world below.

Set name	
Rattlecopter	
Year	2012
Number	9443
Pieces	327
Minifigures	3

FANGTOM

This Fangpyre general grew a second head when he accidentally bit himself. Fangtom's two heads often finish each other's sentences!

▼ FANGPYRE MECH

It's not only the ninja who fight with mechs. The Serpentine have developed a Fangpyre Mech of their own. Its robotic arms launch poisonous flick-fire missiles, and its grabbing hands snatch up its victims.

FANGDAM

Fangdam serves as the deputy to his brother, Fangtom. His second head is a result of being bitten by Fang-Suei during a fight.

▼ WRECKING BALL

This beast of a vehicle is the most destructive of all in the Serpentine fleet. The Fangpyre Wrecking Ball crane rolls into enemy territory on treads, lowers the wrecking ball with an adjustable winch, then swings its reptilian body to destroy everything in its path.

Winch lever

Set name	
Fangpyre Wrecking Ball	
Year	2012
Number	9457
Pieces	415
Minifigures	3

Floodlight

Wrecking ball

Flexible tail

Snapping snake head

Rolling tread

Crane cockpit

Fang-Suei in the cockpit

Set name	*Fangpyre Mech*	
Year 2012	**Number** 9455	
Pieces 255	**Minifigures** 2	

Razor sharp fangs

Swiveling feet

SNAPPA

This Fangpyre scout's angry expression shows that he is Snappa by name, snappy by nature! The angry asp's red-and-white hood piece snakes down his back like a tail.

FANG-SUEI

Fang-Suei is the strongest Fangpyre soldier of all. Look out for his enormous white fangs. He is always eager to sink them into fresh meat, or candy.

Head spike

◀ SKALIDOR

Skalidor is a real heavyweight in the snake world, in both status and size. He is the leader of the Constrictai and has large, imposing features. Skalidor gained weight during centuries of confinement, and he still gets little exercise.

Double-headed ax

Constrictai Fang blade

Powerful neck

SNIKE

Snike is a hard-working scout and sniper specialist for the Constrictai. He is rarely seen, but when observed Snike will often be carrying one of his tribe's impressive blades.

CHOKUN

The Constrictai value brawn over brains, so slender Chokun finds it hard to stand out as a fighter. His small (for a Serpentine) head features silver scales and huge fangs.

BYTAR

This stocky Constrictai warrior is known for his great strength. Bytar can beat any Serpentine in a tail-wrestling match. Like all Constrictai (apart from Skalidor), he has short legs.

Wide belly plate

Set name	Destiny's Bounty	
Year	2012	**Number** 9446
Pieces	684	**Minifigures** 6

One large red eye

RATTLA

Rattla is a Hypnobrai scout whose powers of hypnosis are somewhat lacking. Could it be caused by him having one hypnotic eye bigger than the other?

▶ HYPNOBRAI SNAKE SHRINE

Skales and Slithraa guard this imposing Snake Shrine from the ninja when they come looking for the Hypnobrai Staff, which contains an antidote for their hypnosis. The ninja will need to avoid their scaly foes as well as the toxic waterfall that surrounds the staff's hiding place.

Falling venom

SLITHRAA

Slithraa used to be the Hypnobrai General until his second-in-command, Skales, seized the title and demoted him to the rank of warrior.

Unique snakeskin pattern

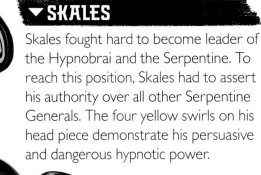

▼ SKALES

Skales fought hard to become leader of the Hypnobrai and the Serpentine. To reach this position, Skales had to assert his authority over all other Serpentine Generals. The four yellow swirls on his head piece demonstrate his persuasive and dangerous hypnotic power.

MEZMO

This assertive and strategic-minded Hypnobrai soldier always speaks his mind, so you cross him at your peril!

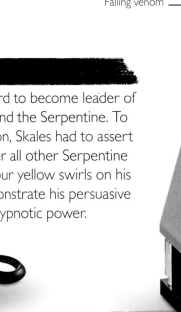

THE STONE ARMY

The legendary Stone Army had not been seen in Ninjago since the time of the First Spinjitzu Master, until some sneaky snakes accidentally unearthed it beneath Ninjago City! The Overlord himself created this force from indestructible Dark Materials buried deep underground. Now it's up to the ninja to bury this ancient enemy once and for all!

▶ GARMATRON

The reawakened Stone Army has work to do building the ultimate weapon—the Garmatron. Lord Garmadon has taken control of the stone soldiers and commanded them to construct the unbeatable battle machine. The Garmatron blasts Dark Matter missiles from its front cannon to infect all of Ninjago with harmful energy.

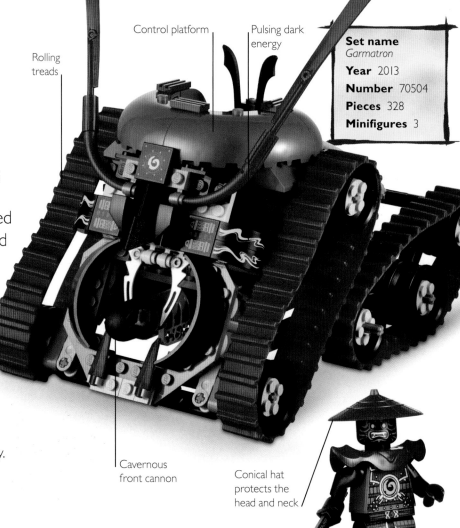

Control platform

Rolling treads

Pulsing dark energy

Set name
Garmatron
Year 2013
Number 70504
Pieces 328
Minifigures 3

Cavernous front cannon

Conical hat protects the head and neck

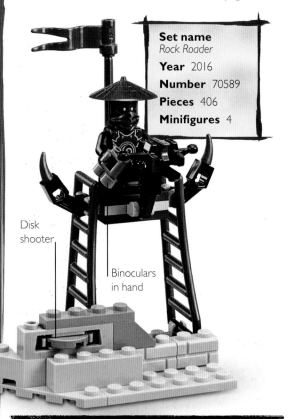

Set name
Rock Roader
Year 2016
Number 70589
Pieces 406
Minifigures 4

Disk shooter

Binoculars in hand

▲ BASE CAMP

At base camp, a Scout is perched at the lookout point with a crossbow in one hand and a pair of binoculars in the other. The Scout is hoping to spy the ninja so that he can activate the camp's secret disk shooter. No one ever sees this coming!

Scimitar sword

GENERAL KOZU

His all-red body armor and imposing horned helmet mark General Kozu as the highest-ranking member of the stone fighters. This fearsome, four-armed warrior is Lord Garmadon's second-in-command.

SWORDSMAN

A Swordsman serves on the front line in battle and is a master with a katana sword. His torso and thigh guards protect him if he finds himself at the sharp end of an enemy's sword.

SCOUT

This Scout is one of the force's lowest-ranking members. Unlike higher-ranking soldiers, he wears no protective shoulder armor. He will need to be a sharp shot with his crossbow to survive a ninja battle!

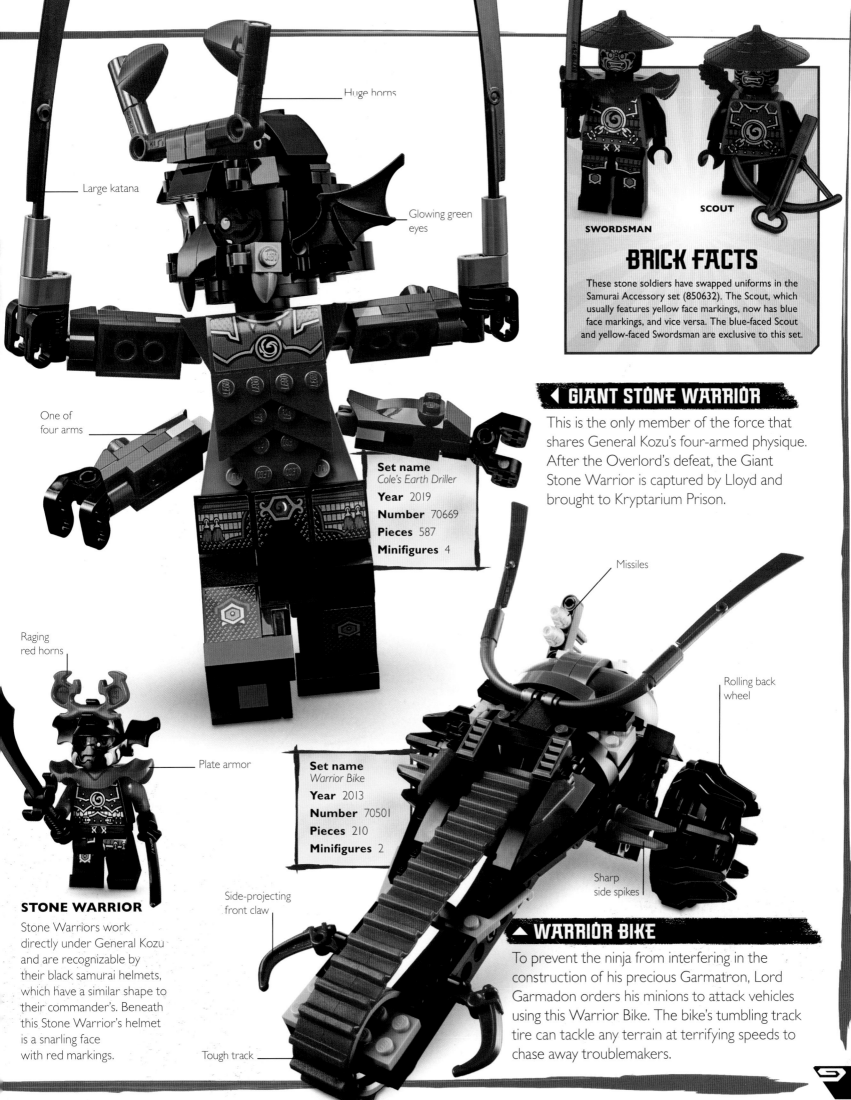

Huge horns

Large katana

Glowing green eyes

One of four arms

Set name
Cole's Earth Driller
Year 2019
Number 70669
Pieces 587
Minifigures 4

Raging red horns

Plate armor

Set name
Warrior Bike
Year 2013
Number 70501
Pieces 210
Minifigures 2

Side-projecting front claw

Tough track

STONE WARRIOR

Stone Warriors work directly under General Kozu and are recognizable by their black samurai helmets, which have a similar shape to their commander's. Beneath this Stone Warrior's helmet is a snarling face with red markings.

SWORDSMAN

SCOUT

BRICK FACTS

These stone soldiers have swapped uniforms in the Samurai Accessory set (850632). The Scout, which usually features yellow face markings, now has blue face markings, and vice versa. The blue-faced Scout and yellow-faced Swordsman are exclusive to this set.

◀ GIANT STONE WARRIOR

This is the only member of the force that shares General Kozu's four-armed physique. After the Overlord's defeat, the Giant Stone Warrior is captured by Lloyd and brought to Kryptarium Prison.

Missiles

Rolling back wheel

Sharp side spikes

▲ WARRIOR BIKE

To prevent the ninja from interfering in the construction of his precious Garmatron, Lord Garmadon orders his minions to attack vehicles using this Warrior Bike. The bike's tumbling track tire can tackle any terrain at terrifying speeds to chase away troublemakers.

NINDROIDS

This breed of ninja enemy is a technological menace. The Nindroids become a force to be reckoned with when their leader, the Overlord, copies the blueprints of Nindroid Zane. The Overlord then builds hundreds of humanoid robots that can do everything Zane can—but as the next generation of Nindroid, they are faster, stronger, and more agile. They also carry out the Overlord's orders without question.

Large flag

Laser cannon

Bonelike bars surround cockpit area

The Overlord's bladed weapon

Legs crawl like a spider's legs

Set name	*Battle for Ninjago City*	
Year 2014	**Number** 70728	
Pieces 1,223	**Minifigures** 8	

Crooked teeth

Two pairs of arms

THE OVERLORD

Sporting four arms and super-crooked teeth, the Overlord in spirit form looks truly sinister. It's no surprise that he's one of the toughest opponents the ninja have to face.

▶ OVERLORD MECH

The Overlord is a supreme nuisance to the ninja. For a long time, he exists as a spirit, then he takes physical form. When this happens, he gets around using a mech with three spiderlike legs. The mech is armed with a laser cannon, so don't mess with it!

Saw blade

Mechanical headpiece

Artificial arm

◀ CYRUS BORG

Disabled from birth, genius inventor Cyrus Borg created his own artificial limbs. He also helps build the futuristic metropolis of New Ninjago City. When the Overlord becomes a computer virus, he transforms unsuspecting Borg into a villainous cyborg called the OverBorg. He is programmed to return the Overlord to a living body.

Exhaust pipe

Set name	
OverBorg Attack	
Year 2014	
Number 70722	
Pieces 207	
Minifigures 2	

Mech chair attachment

One of six mechanical legs

▶ TANK BIKE

The OverBorg can only get so far on his artificial limbs. When he needs to tear up the road to catch a ninja, he attaches his mechanical chair to this tank bike. It has an all-terrain tread tire and slicing saw blades.

Dagger

Set name	*OverBorg Attack*	
Year 2014	**Number** 70722	
Pieces 207	**Minifigures** 2	

Computer interface

Set name
NinjaCopter
Year 2014
Number 70724
Pieces 516
Minifigures 4

Jet
engine

◀ **JET FIGHTER**

This Nindroid Warrior can both soar and saw in his jet fighter with built-in saw blade propellers. The high-tech computer inside its cockpit allows him to communicate with troops on the ground.

Tail fin

Set name
NinjaCopter
Year 2014
Number 70724
Pieces 516
Minifigures 4

Nindroid Drone, the lowest-ranking member of the Nindroid Army

Starboard wing

▶ **GLIDER**

This glider detaches from the rear of the Nindroid Jet Fighter to launch a double aerial attack on the NinjaCopter. When its Drone pilot reaches its target, he can whip out one or both of the craft's daggers to take the ninja down.

Saw blade swooshes from side to side

Dagger holder

Saw blade

Shoulder armor

GENERAL CRYPTOR

General Cryptor was the first Nindroid ever created. He is an upgraded version of Zane, with more advanced programming. He is leader of the Nindroid Army.

NINDROID WARRIOR

Armed with his vicious saw blade, this Nindroid Warrior is the ninja's most lethal foe ever. This superior Nindroid can run faster, leap higher, and never gets tired.

NINDROID MACHINES

Borg Tower is the head office of Cyrus Borg's technological empire, Borg Industries, and is located in the heart of New Ninjago City. From here the Overlord and the OverBorg develop a fleet of machines for their Nindroid force. The Overlord uses Borg's brilliant mind to create the most technologically advanced attack vehicles Ninjago has ever seen.

Computerized dashboard

Missile

Saw blade

Rotating metal blade

► HOVER SLICER

This one-man hovercraft is light enough to take any tight corner in New Ninjago City. The ninja can try to run from it, but they cannot hide from its huge spinning saw blade.

Tail light

Handlebar

▲ HOVER HUNTER

The Hover Hunter's huge front saw blade acts as both a propeller and a weapon, allowing its Nindroid pilot to rip up the streets of Ninjago in all senses of the phrase!

Detachable sword

Jet booster

NINDROID JETPACK

When a Nindroid straps on a jetpack and takes to the skies, he targets Zane's Titanium Ninja Tumbler. The jetpack is small, but the Nindroid carries a missile launcher that could do some serious damage!

Wing blade

Control column

► JETPACK

A Nindroid Warrior can control the height and direction of this advanced jetpack using the control column to his left side.

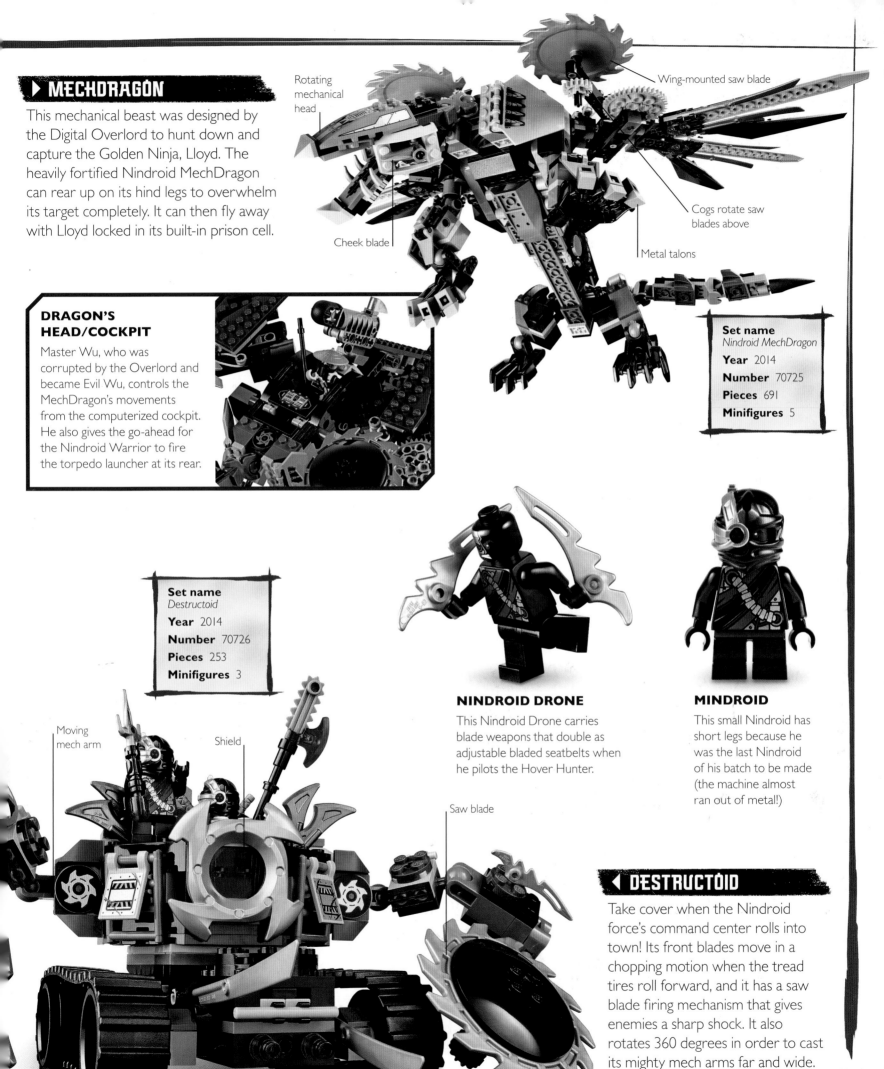

▶ MECHDRAGON

This mechanical beast was designed by the Digital Overlord to hunt down and capture the Golden Ninja, Lloyd. The heavily fortified Nindroid MechDragon can rear up on its hind legs to overwhelm its target completely. It can then fly away with Lloyd locked in its built-in prison cell.

Rotating mechanical head

Wing-mounted saw blade

Cogs rotate saw blades above

Cheek blade

Metal talons

DRAGON'S HEAD/COCKPIT

Master Wu, who was corrupted by the Overlord and became Evil Wu, controls the MechDragon's movements from the computerized cockpit. He also gives the go-ahead for the Nindroid Warrior to fire the torpedo launcher at its rear.

Set name
Nindroid MechDragon
Year 2014
Number 70725
Pieces 691
Minifigures 5

Set name
Destructoid
Year 2014
Number 70726
Pieces 253
Minifigures 3

Moving mech arm

Shield

NINDROID DRONE

This Nindroid Drone carries blade weapons that double as adjustable bladed seatbelts when he pilots the Hover Hunter.

MINDROID

This small Nindroid has short legs because he was the last Nindroid of his batch to be made (the machine almost ran out of metal!)

Saw blade

◀ DESTRUCTOID

Take cover when the Nindroid force's command center rolls into town! Its front blades move in a chopping motion when the tread tires roll forward, and it has a saw blade firing mechanism that gives enemies a sharp shock. It also rotates 360 degrees in order to cast its mighty mech arms far and wide.

TOURNAMENT OF ELEMENTS

Master Chen—the owner of a successful chain of noodle restaurants—sends the ninja a mysterious message. He invites them to compete in the Tournament of Elements. When the ninja arrive on Chen's island, they discover Chen isn't planning to fight fair!

Set name	Jungle Trap	
Year 2015	**Number**	70752
Pieces 58	**Minifigures**	2

Slashing swords

Trap step

Tropical leaves

Helmet resembles Anacondrai skull

CHEN

Master Chen is the ringleader of a secret criminal empire. He organizes the Tournament of Elements as an elaborate scheme to steal the powers of the Elemental Masters and use them to convert his followers into Anacondrai warriors.

▲ JUNGLE TRAP

This Tournament of Elements challenge is especially tricky—if Kai accidentally walks on the trap step, two slashing swords will be activated and the tournament will be over for him. Fortunately, Kai doesn't make that mistake and reaches the Jade Blade prize.

▼ LAVA FALLS

One of Master Chen's dastardly challenges is making the contestents battle each other on a flimsy bridge that crosses over a molten lava pit in a volcano! The first contestant to make it over the bridge gets a Jade Blade and progresses to the next stage of the tournament.

Set name
Lava Falls
Year 2015
Number 70753
Pieces 94
Minifigures 2

Jade Blade

Fire from molten lava pit

Broken bridge

Bow and arrow

Spear

Sushi roll slice

SKYLOR

Skylor is Master Chen's daughter. When she realizes her father is a villain, she sides with the ninja. Skylar inherited the title of Elemental Master of Amber from her mother.

CLOUSE

The Master of Dark Arts, Clouse is Master Chen's deputy and helps organize the Tournament of Elements. This suspicious character keeps a close eye on the ninja.

Shuriken
in belt

Powerful
metal glove

Smoke
bomb

Scimitar

GRIFFIN

Speedy Griffin Turner
is the Elemental Master
of Speed. He competes
against the ninja in the
Tournament of Elements,
but later joins them in
their battle against Chen.

KARLOF

The Elemental Master of
Metal, Karlof also competes
in the tournament. After
being defeated by Kai, Karlof
teams up with Cole to free
a group of workers being
held prisoner on the island.

ASH

Ash is the Elemental
Master of Smoke. During
the Tournament of
Elements, Ash fights
Kai inside a volcano. The
heat is on for a battle
between Fire and Smoke!

SHADE

Stealthy Shade is a tough
contestant. He is the
Elemental Master of
Shadow, until Master Chen
strips him of his powers. He
helps the ninja to defeat
Chen and regain his powers.

▶ DOJO SHOWDOWN

The ninja need to be at their very
best to stand a chance of winning
the Tournament of Elements. Our
heroes end up in the dojo trying to
counter Karlof's metal fists and
Griffin Turner's speed. The ninja's
speed and agility help them avoid
the dangerous spinning blade bot
in their path!

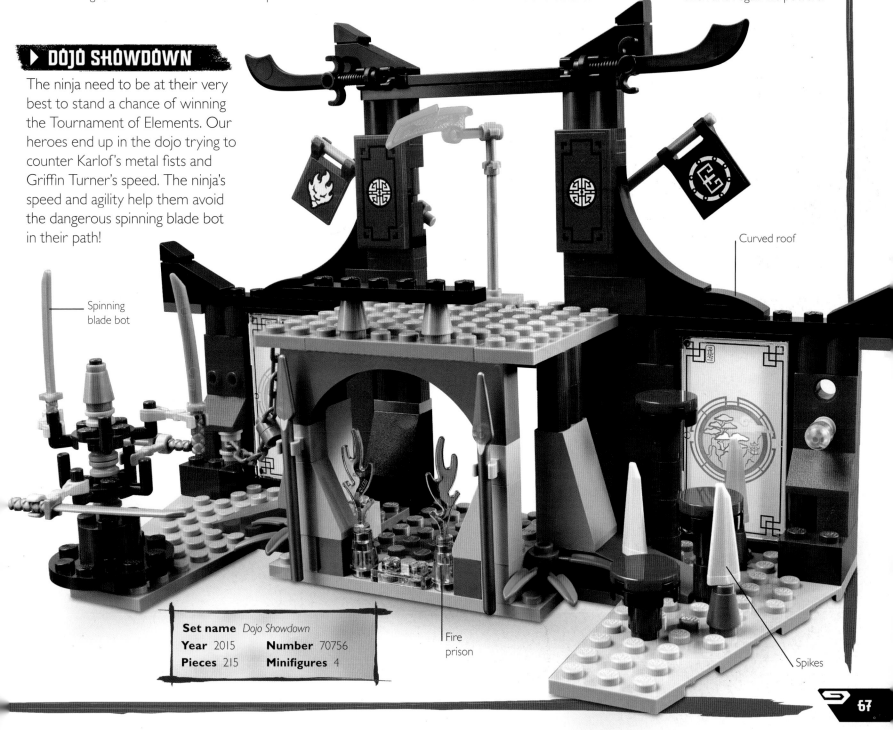

Curved roof

Spinning
blade bot

Fire
prison

Spikes

Set name	Dojo Showdown	
Year	2015	Number 70756
Pieces	215	Minifigures 4

ANACONDRAI

Master Chen has gathered a group of followers on a secluded island. They worship an ancient Serpentine tribe called the Anacondrai. Chen plots to use Pythor—the last living Anacondrai—and the ninja's elemental powers to transform his followers into new Anacondrai warriors. When they threaten to invade Ninjago Island, it's up to the Elemental Masters and their friends to stop the fake snakes!

Set name
Condrai Copter Attack
Year 2015
Number 70746
Pieces 311
Minifigures 3

Mohawk haircut

EYEZOR

Eyezor is the General of Master Chen's Anacondrai worshippers. He often makes mischief with Sleven and Krait. When he becomes an Anacondrai, he changes his name to Eyezorai.

ZUGU

A former Sumo wrestler, Zugo becomes one of Chen's generals. He works in Chen's Underground Noodle Factory before transforming into an Anacondrai with the name of Zugurai.

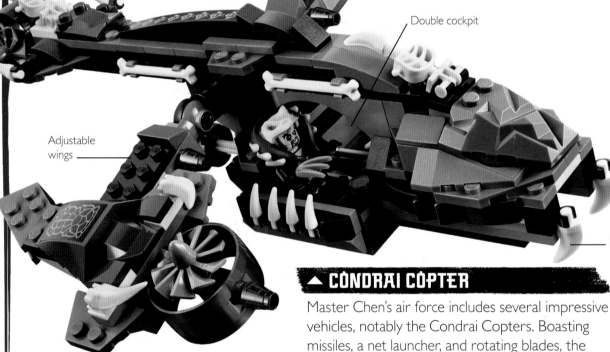

Double cockpit

Adjustable wings

Fangs

Anacondrai markings

KRAIT

As one of Chen's henchmen, Krait is a ruthless fighter totally dedicated to his master's cause. When he transforms into an Anacondrai, Krait changes his name to Krait'rai.

▲ CONDRAI COPTER

Master Chen's air force includes several impressive vehicles, notably the Condrai Copters. Boasting missiles, a net launcher, and rotating blades, the Copters have wings that can go from flight to attack mode in a nanosecond. These smart aircraft are used to keep watch on the island's visitors.

CHOPE

Chope is one of Chen's Anacondrai foot-soldiers. He is ambitious, and he thinks that the way to rise up in the ranks is to have a cool nickname.

Hollowed-out Anacondrai skull

KAPAU

Kapau shares his friend Chope's obsession with having a cool name. As an Anacondrai, he becomes Kapau'rai. Like Chope, Kapau wants to move up the ranks.

SLEVEN

Sleven divides his time between defending Chen's island and delivering noodles for Chen's Noodle Factory. As an Anacondrai warrior, his name is Slevenrai.

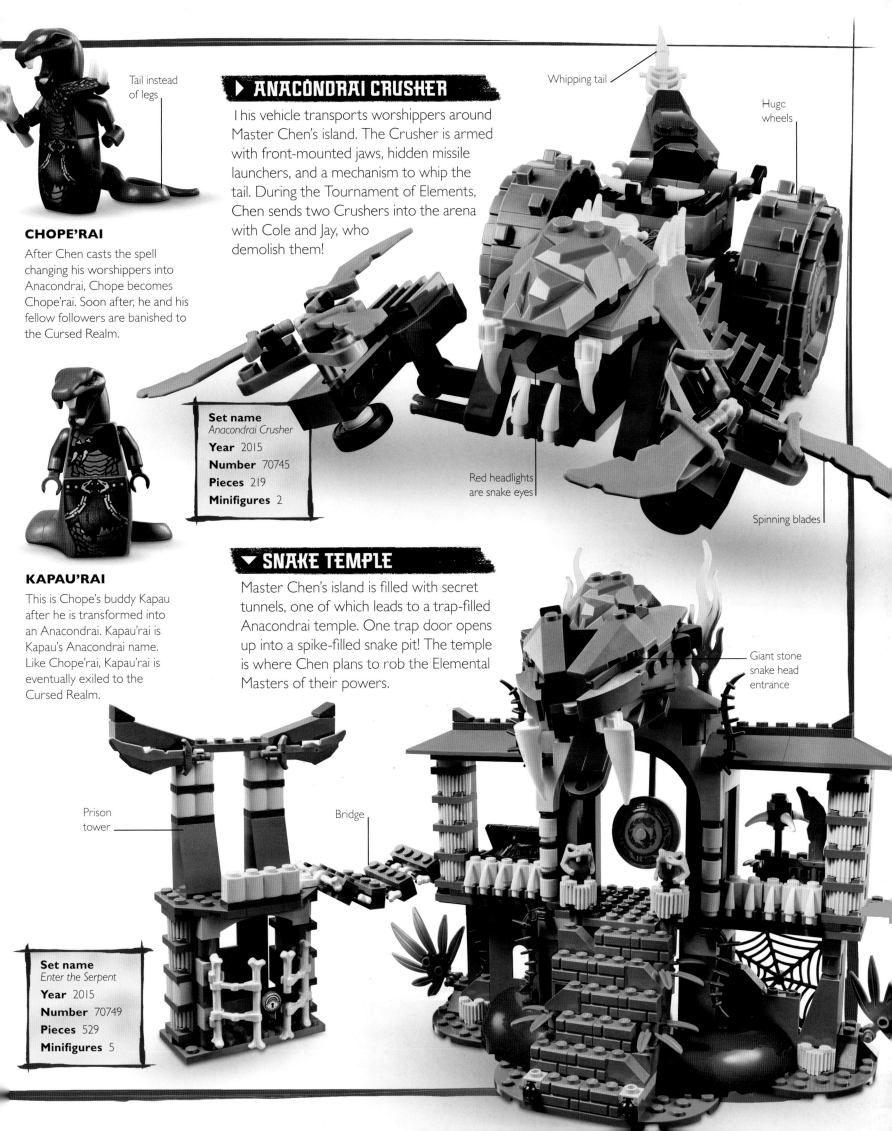

CHOPE'RAI

Tail instead of legs

After Chen casts the spell changing his worshippers into Anacondrai, Chope becomes Chope'rai. Soon after, he and his fellow followers are banished to the Cursed Realm.

KAPAU'RAI

This is Chope's buddy Kapau after he is transformed into an Anacondrai. Kapau'rai is Kapau's Anacondrai name. Like Chope'rai, Kapau'rai is eventually exiled to the Cursed Realm.

▶ ANACONDRAI CRUSHER

This vehicle transports worshippers around Master Chen's island. The Crusher is armed with front-mounted jaws, hidden missile launchers, and a mechanism to whip the tail. During the Tournament of Elements, Chen sends two Crushers into the arena with Cole and Jay, who demolish them!

Whipping tail

Huge wheels

Red headlights are snake eyes

Spinning blades

Set name
Anacondrai Crusher
Year 2015
Number 70745
Pieces 219
Minifigures 2

▼ SNAKE TEMPLE

Master Chen's island is filled with secret tunnels, one of which leads to a trap-filled Anacondrai temple. One trap door opens up into a spike-filled snake pit! The temple is where Chen plans to rob the Elemental Masters of their powers.

Giant stone snake head entrance

Prison tower

Bridge

Set name
Enter the Serpent
Year 2015
Number 70749
Pieces 529
Minifigures 5

THE GHOST NINJA

A group of ghosts has invaded Ninjago, and it's led by Master Wu's first pupil! Years ago, Morro failed to become the Green Ninja. He went to the Caves of Despair, where his spirit was banished to the Cursed Realm. Now, Morro's ghost is back in Ninjago and wants revenge. He creates a band of ghosts to help him, and even tries to possess Lloyd!

Green, glowing skin

Double-bladed scythe

Tattered cape

SCYTHE MASTER GHOULTAR

Ghoultar is a powerful ghost and Morro's loyal lieutenant. However, he is easily distracted, and isn't that bright. He likes Chen's Puffy Potstickers and music.

BOW MASTER SOUL ARCHER

Soul Archer's arrows can transform their targets into ghosts! Soul Archer is calm in a crisis and often offers advice to his leader, Morro.

▲ MORRO

The Elemental Master of Wind, Morro has many skills. He is devastated when the Golden Weapons of Spinjitzu do not react to him. Now, Morro seeks to get revenge on his teacher, Master Wu, and the new Green Ninja, Lloyd.

Tail

Lloyd is possessed by Morro

Sickly green wings

Chain to control dragon

EVIL GREEN NINJA

Lloyd is mourning the death of his father, Lord Garmadon, which allows the cursed spirit of Morro to possess him. This now-evil Lloyd turns on his friends, until Morro leaves his body.

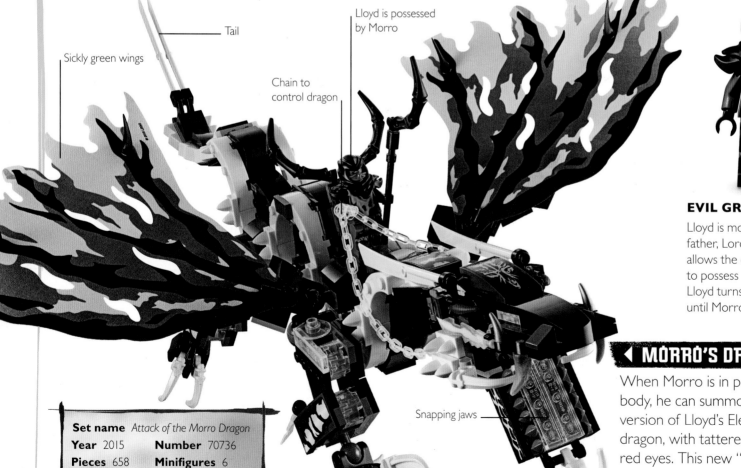

◀ MORRO'S DRAGON

When Morro is in possession of Lloyd's body, he can summon a corrupted version of Lloyd's Elemental Energy dragon, with tattered wings and glowing red eyes. This new "Morro Dragon" is used to attack the other ninja.

Snapping jaws

Set name *Attack of the Morro Dragon*
Year 2015   Number 70736
Pieces 658   Minifigures 6

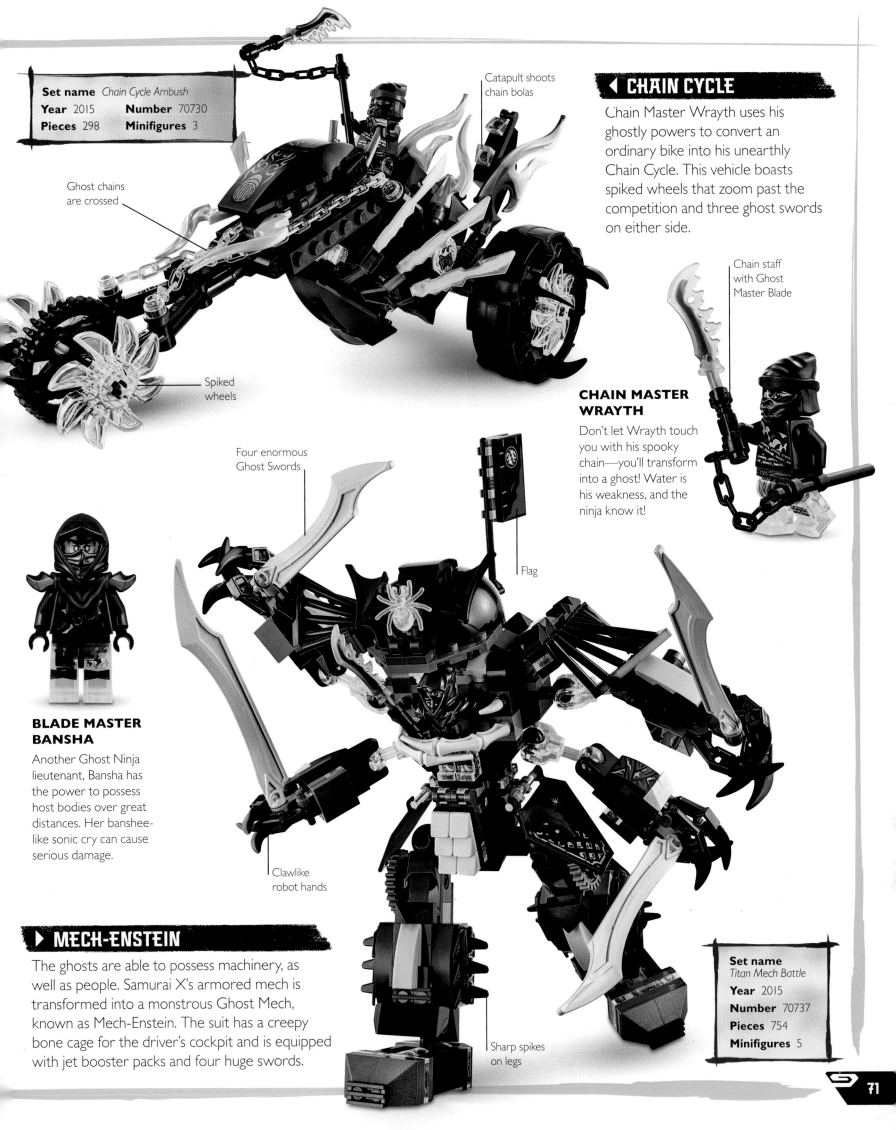

Set name	Chain Cycle Ambush	
Year	2015	Number 70730
Pieces	298	Minifigures 3

Ghost chains
are crossed

Catapult shoots
chain bolas

Chain Master Wrayth uses his ghostly powers to convert an ordinary bike into his unearthly Chain Cycle. This vehicle boasts spiked wheels that zoom past the competition and three ghost swords on either side.

Spiked
wheels

Chain staff
with Ghost
Master Blade

CHAIN MASTER WRAYTH

Don't let Wrayth touch you with his spooky chain—you'll transform into a ghost! Water is his weakness, and the ninja know it!

Four enormous
Ghost Swords

Flag

BLADE MASTER BANSHA

Another Ghost Ninja lieutenant, Bansha has the power to possess host bodies over great distances. Her banshee-like sonic cry can cause serious damage.

Clawlike
robot hands

▶ MECH-ENSTEIN

The ghosts are able to possess machinery, as well as people. Samurai X's armored mech is transformed into a monstrous Ghost Mech, known as Mech-Enstein. The suit has a creepy bone cage for the driver's cockpit and is equipped with jet booster packs and four huge swords.

Sharp spikes
on legs

Set name	
Titan Mech Battle	
Year	2015
Number	70737
Pieces	754
Minifigures	5

GHOST TOWN

Morro is able to free a large number of ghostly followers—and mischievous Skreemers—from the Cursed Realm. As Morro's ghosts spread across Ninjago Island, more people and places fall under his control, including the City of Stiix. Morro eventually releases the most powerful ghost of all: the Preeminent. It is up to the ninja to save the city and send the ghosts back to their own realm!

Spooky sail

Set name
City of Stiix
Year 2015
Number 70732
Pieces 1,069
Minifigures 9

Decoration resembles Cowler's hat

BRICK FACTS

Skreemers are small, loud, and hungry bundles of ghostly energy. The Skreemer minifigure included in City of Stiix (set 70732) also featured in Chain Cycle Ambush (set 70730).

▶ GHOST SHIP

Morro's Ghost Ship sails across the night sky, fueled by phantom energy. The boat itself has been infected with the ghostly characteristics of its crew. The ninja must avoid getting caught and trapped in the onboard prison.

Front blade

Hull

Cannon

▶ POSSESSED RICKSHAW

Morro's Ghost Warriors will do anything to transform the population of Ninjago into ghosts. Ghost Warrior Pitch disguises himself as a snack seller. Watch out for the treats this rickshaw is selling though—they're part of a trick!

Ghost crystal can infect others

Hidden ghost disk shooter

Pitch's pitchfork

Set name
Master Wu Dragon
Year 2015
Number 70734
Pieces 575
Minifigures 5

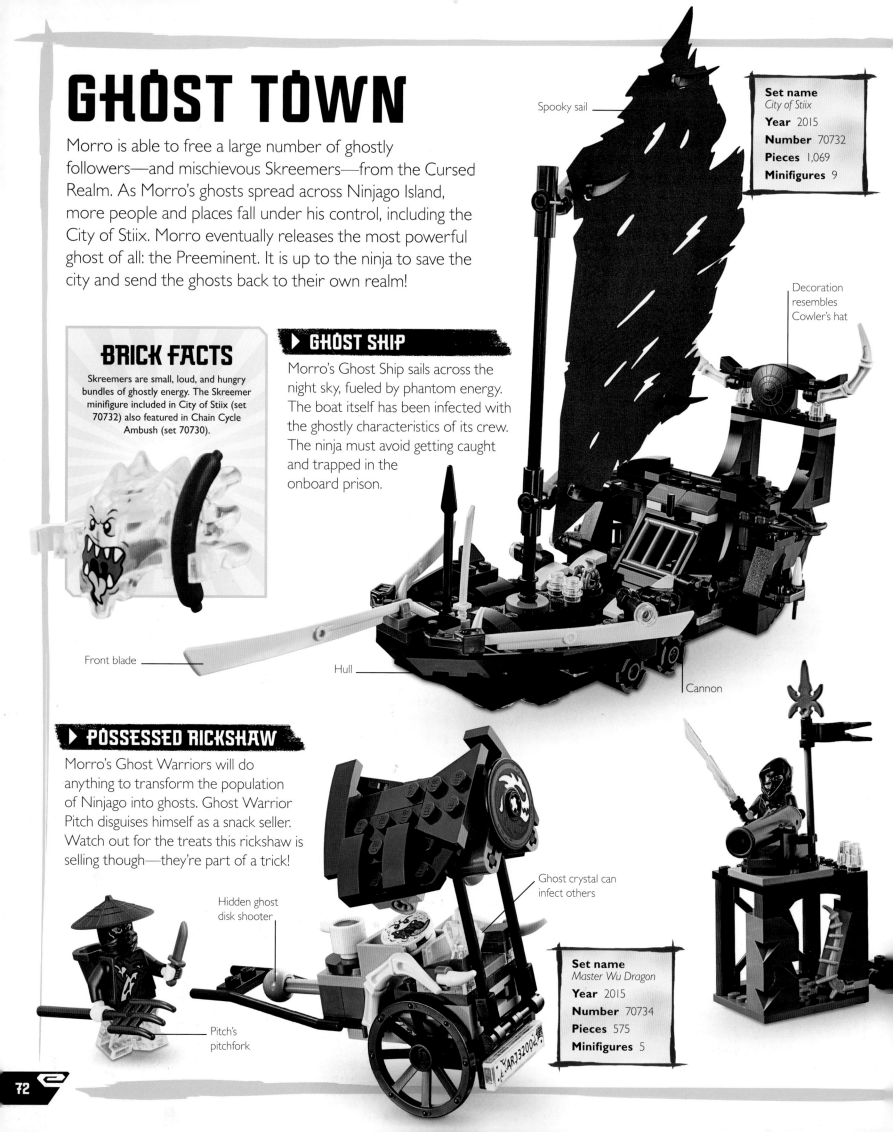

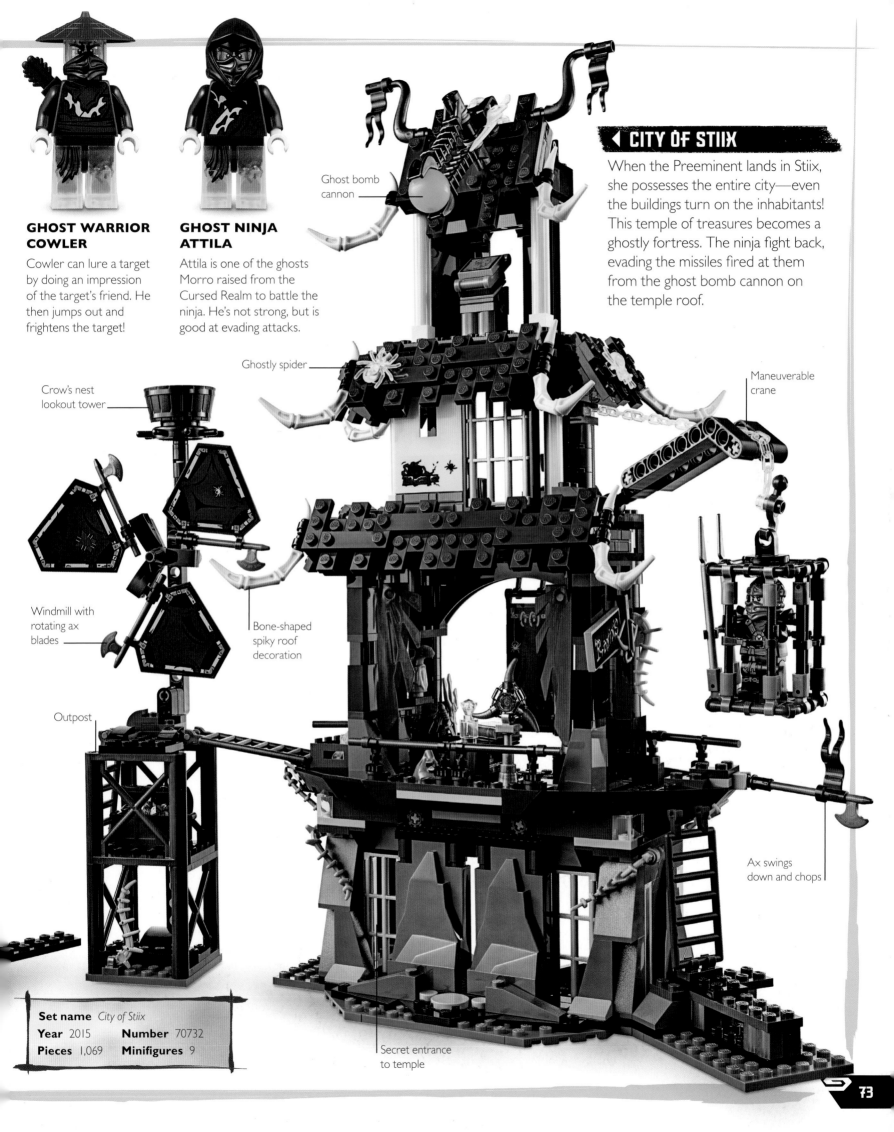

GHOST WARRIOR COWLER

Cowler can lure a target by doing an impression of the target's friend. He then jumps out and frightens the target!

GHOST NINJA ATTILA

Attila is one of the ghosts Morro raised from the Cursed Realm to battle the ninja. He's not strong, but is good at evading attacks.

Ghost bomb cannon

Ghostly spider

Crow's nest lookout tower

Windmill with rotating ax blades

Outpost

◄ CITY OF STIIX

When the Preeminent lands in Stiix, she possesses the entire city—even the buildings turn on the inhabitants! This temple of treasures becomes a ghostly fortress. The ninja fight back, evading the missiles fired at them from the ghost bomb cannon on the temple roof.

Maneuverable crane

Bone-shaped spiky roof decoration

Ax swings down and chops

Secret entrance to temple

Set name *City of Stiix*
Year 2015   **Number** 70732
Pieces 1,069   **Minifigures** 9

SKY PIRATES

Long ago, a crew of pirates led by their captain, Nadakhan, sailed the Ninjago seas aboard a ship called *Misfortune's Keep*. But the pirates were attacked, Nadakhan was trapped in the Teapot of Tyrahn, and his crew were scattered to other realms! When Nadakhan finally escaped from the teapot, he gathered his crew back together and set forth on a new campaign of crime.

Set name
Jay's Elemental Dragon
Year 2016
Number 70602
Pieces 350
Minifigures 2

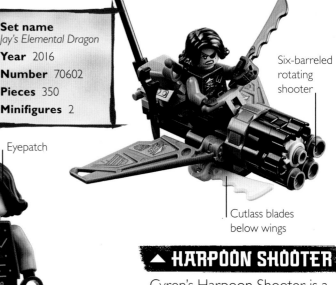

Six-barreled rotating shooter

Cutlass blades below wings

Eyepatch

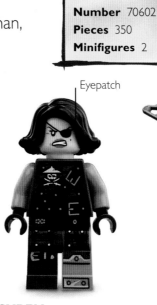

◀ NADAKHAN

Nadakhan is a Djinn, a magical being who can grant wishes. He masterminds a scheme to tear Ninjago apart with the help of his pirate crew. This time he plans to take to the skies, rather than the seas!

CYREN

Sky Pirate Cyren wants to be the world's best singer. Nadakhan grants her wish by giving her a voice that sends those who hear it into a trance. The result is that her voice is her greatest weapon!

▲ HARPOON SHOOTER

Cyren's Harpoon Shooter is a tiny, one-seat airship armed with a six-barreled shooter. Cyren proudly flies the Sky Pirates flag from the back of her ship.

Aerodynamic rear fin

Nadakhan floats and flies around

▶ MISFORTUNE'S KEEP

Originally, Nadakhan's ship is only a seagoing vessel. However, when Nadakhan escapes from the Teapot of Tyrahn and frees his crew, the ship is converted into a flying vessel. It's fast and equipped with several cannons.

Exhaust pipe

Rotor blades shaped like pirate swords

Jay fends off Nadakhan's attack

Set name
Misfortune's Keep
Year 2016
Number 70605
Pieces 754
Minifigures 6

FLINTLOCKE

Meet Flintlocke, Nadakhan's loyal First Mate. The buckles and harnesses on Flintlocke's outfit show that he's a seasoned pirate who's spent a lot of time at sea.

▶ SKY SHARK

The Sky Shark is a high-tech jet that flies ahead of *Misfortune's Keep* to look out for any airborne threats to the Sky Pirates. Its anchor-shaped wings are sharp enough to cut through steel. The jet's cargo of dynamite can be dropped onto other aircraft.

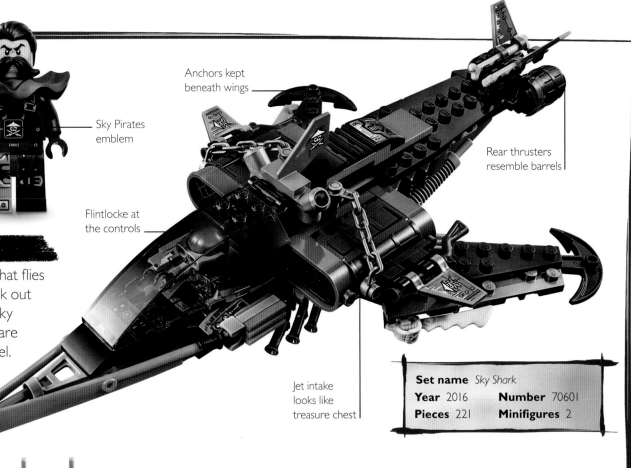

Anchors kept beneath wings

Sky Pirates emblem

Rear thrusters resemble barrels

Flintlocke at the controls

Jet intake looks like treasure chest

Set name	*Sky Shark*		
Year 2016		**Number** 70601	
Pieces 221		**Minifigures** 2	

Samurai helmet

Set name	
Raid Zeppelin	
Year 2016	
Number 70603	
Pieces 294	
Minifigures 3	

Balloon keeps craft airborne

CLANCEE

Clancee is a green, scaly Serpentine and the most useless pirate in Nadakhan's crew! He is only on *Misfortune's Keep* because another pirate fell overboard.

DOUBLOON

Doubloon is a chatty escape artist and burglar. Nadakhan turns the talkative thief into a mute pirate with two faces. He is a brilliant swordsman and a former student of Spinjitzu.

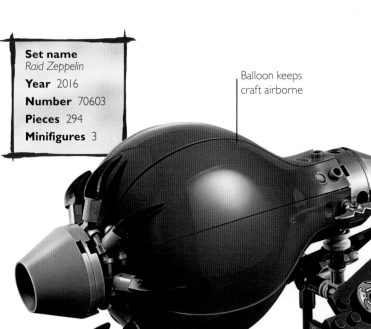

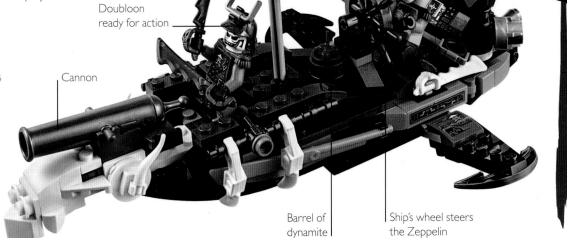

Doubloon ready for action

▶ RAID ZEPPELIN

One of the most formidable vehicles used by the Sky Pirates, the Raid Zeppelin is used in raids on coastal towns and cargo ships. The craft is held aloft by a balloon full of hot air, and is piloted using a wheel. It's armed with a cannon at the bow.

Cannon

Barrel of dynamite

Ship's wheel steers the Zeppelin

SKY PIRATE BASES

The Sky Pirates are, by definition, a roving band of raiders—they don't have one fixed home. However, they have created bases and fortresses in a number of locations. They have also seized other spaces and turned them into pirate hideouts. But even the best hideaways can't fool the ninja heroes!

▼ TIGER WIDOW ISLAND

Nadakhan traps Lloyd's soul in a sword and hides it on a remote island in the Endless Sea. The island is named after the enormous Tiger Widow spider that lives there, but Cole must also faces hazards such as falling coconuts, angry sand worms, and the giant pirate, Dogshank.

▼ FORT AND CATAPULT

When they end up in a battle with the ninja, the Sky Pirates climb their lookout tower. From there, Bucko orders his men to load a boulder in the catapult. He can rely on the weapon when trying to guard Nadakhan's Djinn Blade against The Elemental Dragon of Energy.

Animal skull on catapult

Set name	The Green NRG Dragon	
Year 2016	Number	70593
Pieces 567	Minifigures	5

Ammunition pile

Sun emblem

Scimitar-shaped decoration

Palm tree

Dogshank

Set name
Tiger Widow Island
Year 2016
Number 70604
Pieces 450
Minifigures 5

Rickety ladder

Lloyd's soul trapped in Djinn Blade

Tiger Widow spider

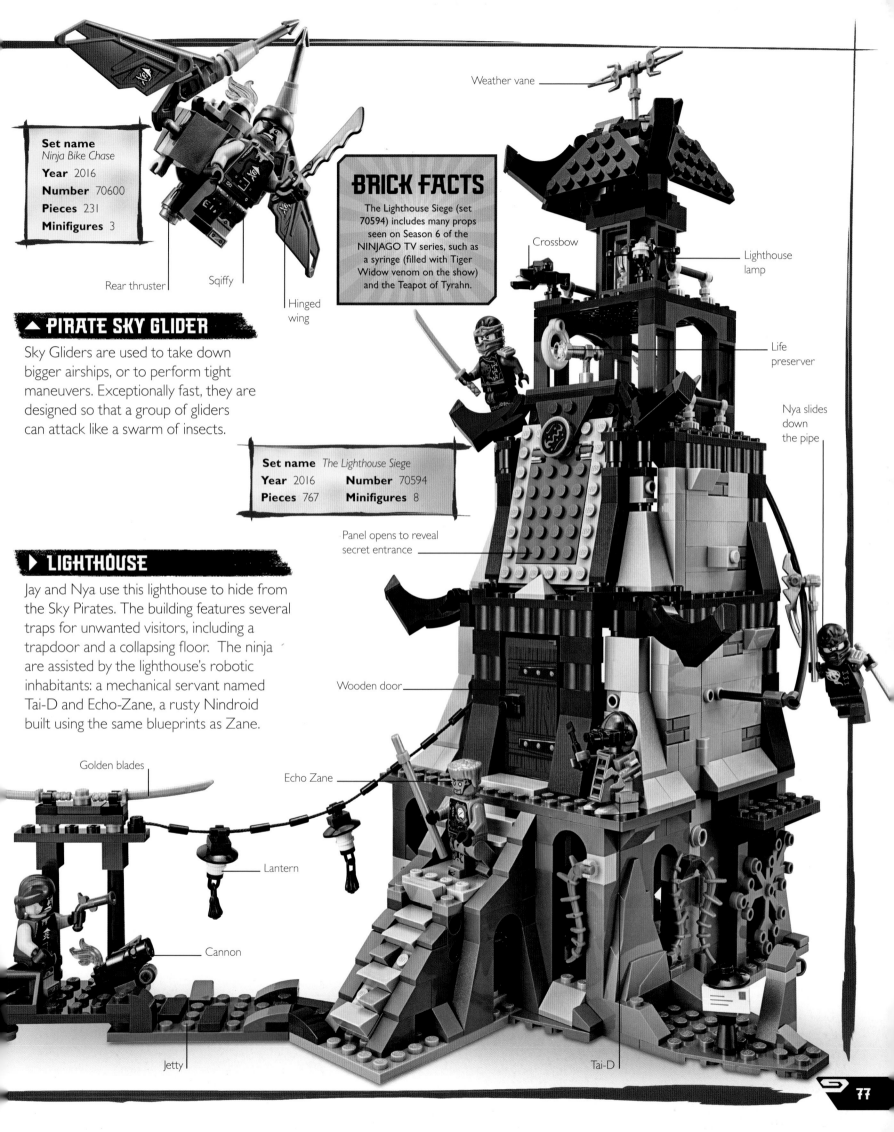

Set name
Ninja Bike Chase
Year 2016
Number 70600
Pieces 231
Minifigures 3

Rear thruster

Sqiffy

Hinged wing

Weather vane

BRICK FACTS

The Lighthouse Siege (set 70594) includes many props seen on Season 6 of the NINJAGO TV series, such as a syringe (filled with Tiger Widow venom on the show) and the Teapot of Tyrahn.

Crossbow

Lighthouse lamp

Life preserver

Nya slides down the pipe

▲ PIRATE SKY GLIDER

Sky Gliders are used to take down bigger airships, or to perform tight maneuvers. Exceptionally fast, they are designed so that a group of gliders can attack like a swarm of insects.

Set name *The Lighthouse Siege*
Year 2016   **Number** 70594
Pieces 767   **Minifigures** 8

Panel opens to reveal secret entrance

▶ LIGHTHOUSE

Jay and Nya use this lighthouse to hide from the Sky Pirates. The building features several traps for unwanted visitors, including a trapdoor and a collapsing floor. The ninja are assisted by the lighthouse's robotic inhabitants: a mechanical servant named Tai-D and Echo-Zane, a rusty Nindroid built using the same blueprints as Zane.

Wooden door

Golden blades

Echo Zane

Lantern

Cannon

Jetty

Tai-D

VERMILLION

It is a fight against time when the ninja battle Krux and Acronix—the Elemental Masters of Time. The brothers have raised a battalion of Vermillion Warriors. These snake-creatures are the descendants of the serpent known as the Great Devourer. Every Vermillion Warrior is actually hundreds of snakes moving together— meaning they can quickly re-form when damaged.

ACRONIX

Acronix has been trapped in a Time Vortex for the past 40 years. When he reappears, he hasn't aged a day. This youthful brother can be identified by the MP3 player he carries.

Gray eyebrows

KRUX

While Acronix was trapped in the Time Vortex, Krux disguised himself as Dr. Sander Saunders and waited for his brother's return. He can be identified by the old-fashioned hourglass he wears.

RAGGMUNK

Commander Raggmunk uses his helmet to control the Vermillion Warriors. Their individual snake parts share one hive mind and thoughts.

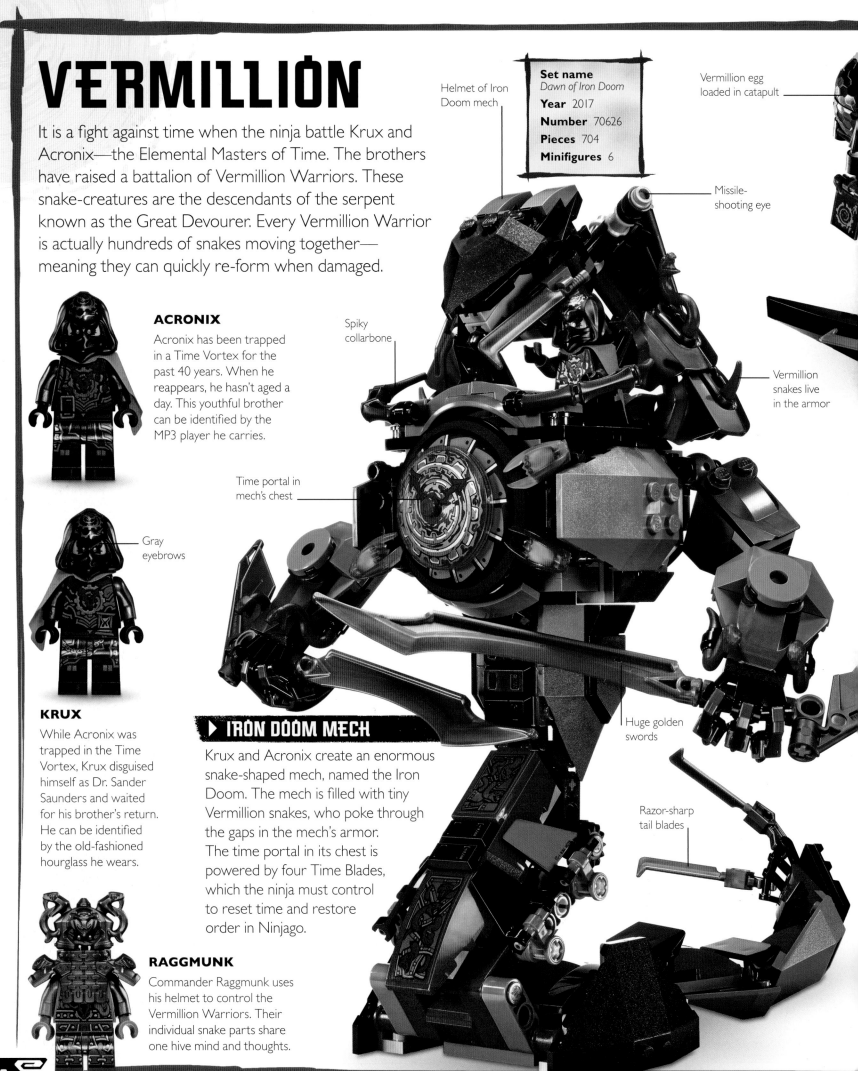

Helmet of Iron Doom mech

Set name *Dawn of Iron Doom*
Year 2017
Number 70626
Pieces 704
Minifigures 6

Vermillion egg loaded in catapult

Missile-shooting eye

Spiky collarbone

Vermillion snakes live in the armor

Time portal in mech's chest

Huge golden swords

▶ IRON DOOM MECH

Krux and Acronix create an enormous snake-shaped mech, named the Iron Doom. The mech is filled with tiny Vermillion snakes, who poke through the gaps in the mech's armor. The time portal in its chest is powered by four Time Blades, which the ninja must control to reset time and restore order in Ninjago.

Razor-sharp tail blades

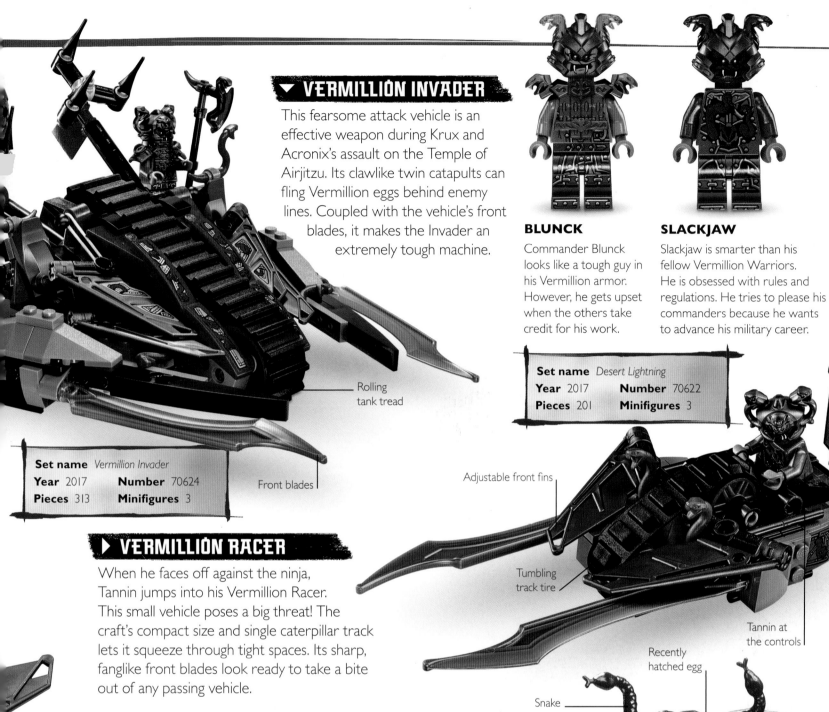

▼ VERMILLION INVADER

This fearsome attack vehicle is an effective weapon during Krux and Acronix's assault on the Temple of Airjitzu. Its clawlike twin catapults can fling Vermillion eggs behind enemy lines. Coupled with the vehicle's front blades, it makes the Invader an extremely tough machine.

Rolling tank tread

Front blades

Set name	Vermillion Invader	
Year	2017	Number 70624
Pieces	313	Minifigures 3

BLUNCK

Commander Blunck looks like a tough guy in his Vermillion armor. However, he gets upset when the others take credit for his work.

SLACKJAW

Slackjaw is smarter than his fellow Vermillion Warriors. He is obsessed with rules and regulations. He tries to please his commanders because he wants to advance his military career.

Set name	Desert Lightning	
Year	2017	Number 70622
Pieces	201	Minifigures 3

▶ VERMILLION RACER

When he faces off against the ninja, Tannin jumps into his Vermillion Racer. This small vehicle poses a big threat! The craft's compact size and single caterpillar track lets it squeeze through tight spaces. Its sharp, fanglike front blades look ready to take a bite out of any passing vehicle.

Adjustable front fins

Tumbling track tire

Tannin at the controls

Armor protects neck and chest

TANNIN

Tannin is even harder to defeat than the other warriors. If a ninja strikes him, Tannin can open his mouth wide and swallow his opponent whole!

RIVETT

Rivett can master any weapon that she holds. Smarter than most warriors, she carries out special missions and can take on several foes at the same time.

▶ VERMILLION EGG

In the Swamplands, Rivett guards a Vermillion egg that is just about to hatch. It is full of tiny baby snakes. Rivett will have to guard it extra carefully since the Forward Time Blade has appeared beside the egg and the ninja will be on their way to find it.

Recently hatched egg

Snake

Forward Time Blade

Set name	
The Vermillion Attack	
Year	2017
Number	70621
Pieces	83
Minifigures	3

SONS OF GARMADON

Villainous biker gang the Sons of Garmadon is made up of criminals from across Ninjago City. New recruits must love high-speed racing, and display the "S.O.G." insignia on their equipment, vehicles, and team jackets. The group is named after Lord Garmadon and is devoted to its mysterious leader, known only as the "Quiet One." The "Quiet One" has ordered the gang to find and steal powerful Oni Masks.

Visor to hide identity

▶ ONI BIKE

The Oni Bike is Mr. E's vehicle. It is armed with two chopping blades, as well as the Sons of Garmadon's trademark red katana swords. Mr. E enjoys taking this large motorcycle on patrol when Garmadon takes over the city.

Button activates chopping motion

Chopping blade

Spikes resemble fangs

Single front wheel

▲ MR. E

Mr. E is a mysterious warrior who never speaks. This silent soldier is actually a Nindroid. However, despite his muted approach to leadership, he is not the "Quiet One".

Set name	Street Race of Snake Jaguar	
Year 2018	**Number** 70639	
Pieces 308	**Minifigures** 2	

Side blades swing out

Spiked baseball bat

Saw blade

KILLOW

Killow is a giant tattooed biker who recruits new members into the Sons of Garmadon. He tests potential new recruits by racing against them in a deadly challenge called "The Teeth."

Set name	
Killow vs. Samurai X	
Year 2018	
Number 70642	
Pieces 556	
Minifigures 3	

▲ ONI CHOPPER

Killow's Oni Chopper is perfect for hunting down enemies, including the ninja. Instead of a front wheel, this mean machine has a saw blade, while side blades swing out to trip up Killow's foes.

Initials on her jacket

ULTRA VIOLET

Ultra Violet is a biker with a wicked sense of humor—although sometimes she is the only one who understands her jokes! She is second-in-command to Mr. E.

ONI MASK ULTRA VIOLET

When Ultra Violet dons her Oni Mask—the Mask of Hatred—her body is covered in a coating of fiery stone, making her temporarily invincible.

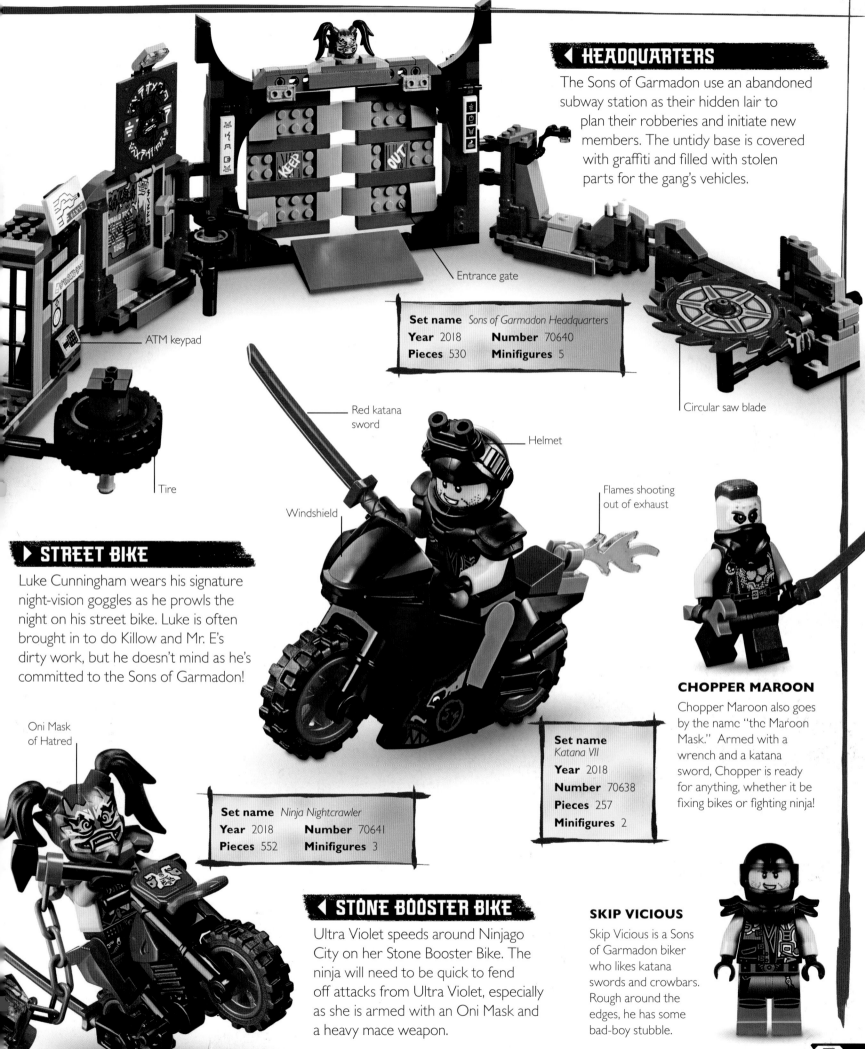

◀ HEADQUARTERS

The Sons of Garmadon use an abandoned subway station as their hidden lair to plan their robberies and initiate new members. The untidy base is covered with graffiti and filled with stolen parts for the gang's vehicles.

ATM keypad

Entrance gate

Set name	Sons of Garmadon Headquarters	
Year 2018	**Number** 70640
Pieces 530	**Minifigures** 5

Circular saw blade

Tire

Red katana sword

Helmet

Windshield

Flames shooting out of exhaust

▶ STREET BIKE

Luke Cunningham wears his signature night-vision goggles as he prowls the night on his street bike. Luke is often brought in to do Killow and Mr. E's dirty work, but he doesn't mind as he's committed to the Sons of Garmadon!

Oni Mask of Hatred

Set name	Ninja Nightcrawler	
Year 2018	**Number** 70641
Pieces 552	**Minifigures** 3

Set name	
Katana VII	
Year 2018	
Number 70638	
Pieces 257	
Minifigures 2	

CHOPPER MAROON

Chopper Maroon also goes by the name "the Maroon Mask." Armed with a wrench and a katana sword, Chopper is ready for anything, whether it be fixing bikes or fighting ninja!

◀ STONE BOOSTER BIKE

Ultra Violet speeds around Ninjago City on her Stone Booster Bike. The ninja will need to be quick to fend off attacks from Ultra Violet, especially as she is armed with an Oni Mask and a heavy mace weapon.

SKIP VICIOUS

Skip Vicious is a Sons of Garmadon biker who likes katana swords and crowbars. Rough around the edges, he has some bad-boy stubble.

ROYAL TROUBLE

The Sons of Garmadon have been trying to steal the powerful Oni Masks from the Ninjago royal family! Princess Harumi decides she needs to hire a team of bodyguards, and Master Wu's pupils are the natural choice! However, the ninja have no idea that the Sons of Garmadon aren't the only enemies they face. The innocent-seeming princess is hiding a secret—and a link to the ninja's oldest foe ...

HUTCHINS

Hutchins serves as the Ninjago royal family's Master-at-Arms. He is loyal and brave, and is willing to defend the royal family with his life if he has to.

PRINCESS HARUMI

With her royal cape and crown, Harumi looks every inch a princess. What isn't obvious to the ninja is that Harumi mistakenly blames them for the deaths of her parents. She believes Lord Garmadon is the real hero of Ninjago City!

— Distinctive white hair

THE QUIET ONE

Princess Harumi has a secret identity. She is the rarely seen "Quiet One" who leads the Sons of Garmadon. It is the Princess who is trying to gather together the Oni Masks.

Lord Garmadon has been resurrected!

Oni Mask

Roof falls in to form angry face —

Lantern —

▶ TEMPLE OF RESURRECTION

Harumi eventually captures all three Oni Masks and reveals that she is the "Quiet One." She takes the trio of masks to the Temple of Resurrection, where she hopes to bring Lord Garmadon back to life. The temple is located in the rocky foundations of the palace, where spiders and other creepy creatures dwell.

Set name	Temple of Resurrection	
Year	2018	Number	70643
Pieces	765	Minifigures	8

Skeleton

Baby is Master Wu!

Prison cell crawling with spiders

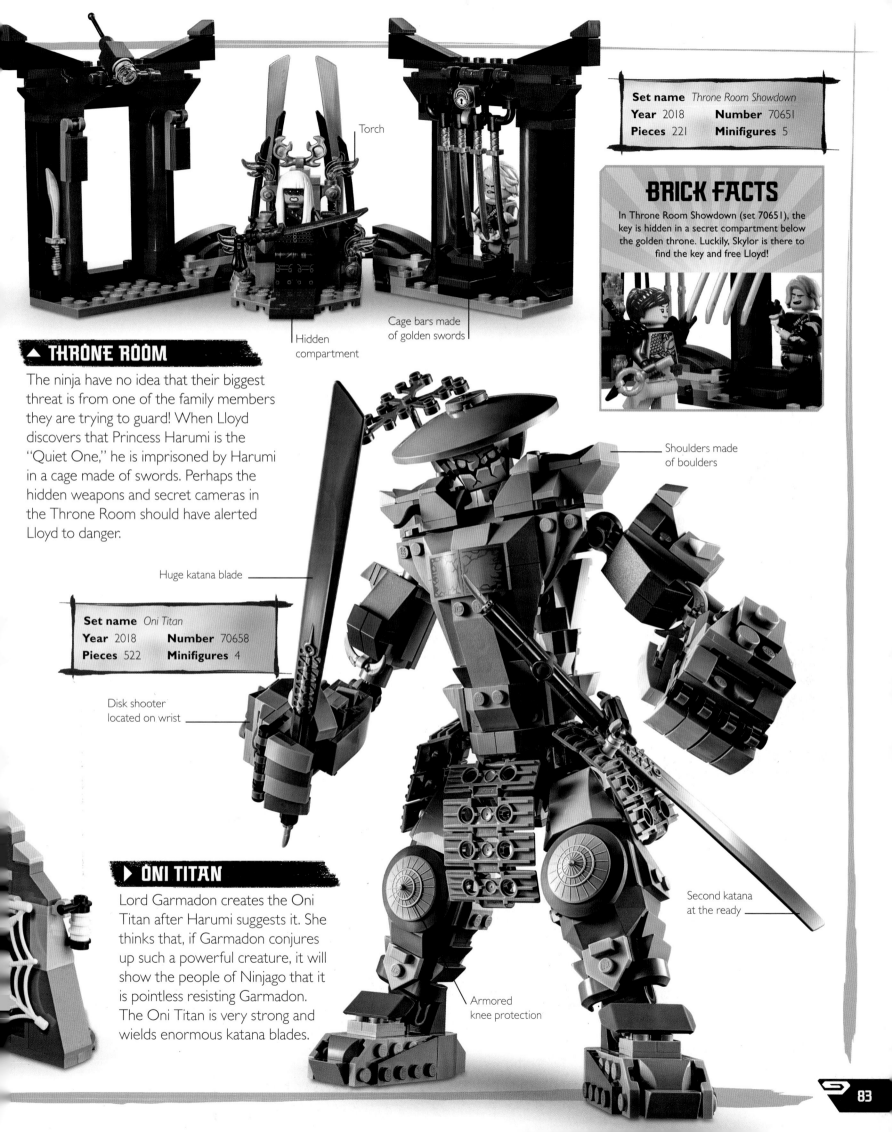

Torch

Hidden compartment

Cage bars made of golden swords

Set name	Throne Room Showdown	
Year 2018		**Number** 70651
Pieces 221		**Minifigures** 5

BRICK FACTS

In Throne Room Showdown (set 70651), the key is hidden in a secret compartment below the golden throne. Luckily, Skylor is there to find the key and free Lloyd!

▲ THRONE ROOM

The ninja have no idea that their biggest threat is from one of the family members they are trying to guard! When Lloyd discovers that Princess Harumi is the "Quiet One," he is imprisoned by Harumi in a cage made of swords. Perhaps the hidden weapons and secret cameras in the Throne Room should have alerted Lloyd to danger.

Shoulders made of boulders

Huge katana blade

Set name	Oni Titan	
Year 2018		**Number** 70658
Pieces 522		**Minifigures** 4

Disk shooter located on wrist

▶ ONI TITAN

Lord Garmadon creates the Oni Titan after Harumi suggests it. She thinks that, if Garmadon conjures up such a powerful creature, it will show the people of Ninjago that it is pointless resisting Garmadon. The Oni Titan is very strong and wields enormous katana blades.

Second katana at the ready

Armored knee protection

DRAGON HUNTERS

The Dragon Hunters live in the First Realm and use their salvaged machinery to hunt dragons—hence their name. Led by the manipulative Iron Baron, they make captured dragons compete in cruel fights. When the ninja are sent to the First Realm, the heroic warriors become the Dragon Hunters' prisoners. Can the ninja free themselves and save the dragons?

Top hat

Cyborg arm

Rear rotor blades made from fangs

▶ IRON BARON

Iron Baron is the leader of the Dragon Hunters. He lies to the members of his own tribe, telling them that he bravely fought Oni, when there are no more Oni in the First Realm. He wears a top hat to show his importance.

▼ DRAGON PIT

When Jay, Kai, and Zane are captured by the Dragon Hunters, they're thrown into a pit and forced to fight a dragon. The tribal warriors keep a sharp eye on the ninja with their watchtower telescope. The sharp dragon fangs on the gates and the pit's jail cell discourage people from attempting to escape.

Shield flanked by dragon claws

Dual missile shooter

Jail cell

Telescope

Throne made from a dragon's skull

Dragon fangs decorate gate

Set name *Dragon Pit*
Year 2018   **Number** 70655
Pieces 1,660   **Minifigures** 9

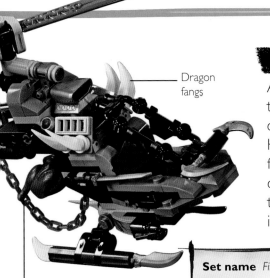

Dragon fangs

Turkey used as bait

◀ HUNTERCOPTER

After coaxing a dragon out into the open, the Dragon Hunters chase the creature with their HunterCopter. Their copter is fully equipped with Vengestone chains, which they can use to tie up the dragon after enticing it with a cooked turkey!

Set name	*Firstbourne*	
Year 2018	**Number**	70653
Pieces 882	**Minifigures**	6

Conical hat

Scarf under grille

MUZZLE

Muzzle is a Dragon Hunter who mumbles and grunts rather than speaks. However, Iron Baron can understand what Muzzle is saying through his metallic mouth grille.

HEAVY METAL

Heavy Metal's real name is Faith. She is Iron Baron's deputy until she allies with the ninja. When Iron Baron is defeated, Faith becomes leader of the Dragon Hunters.

Dragon fang attached to helmet

CHEW TOY

Chew Toy's job is to warm up the crowds before the pit fights where prisoners fight dragons. The toothmarks on his armor suggest that he has got too close to a dragon!

Head wrap hides bandaged face

DADDY NO LEGS

Daddy No Legs transports prisoners to the pit. This Dragon Hunter has a spider-mech instead of legs, so prisoners have to move fast to keep up!

One eye is missing

Spider-mech leg

JET JACK

Jet Jack wants to be Iron Baron's second-in-command. She speeds around the sky using her jetpack hoping to find a dragon. Her aerodynamic haircut won't slow her down!

Mirrored sunglasses

Adjustable wing on jetpack

Crossbow shooter on turret

SKULLBREAKER

Scar the Skullbreaker is another Dragon Hunter who has been injured by his prey. At first he's loyal to Iron Baron, but cheers when his leader is finally defeated.

▶ DIESELNAUT

The Dieselnaut is the Dragon Hunters' main vehicle. This impressive tank has a rotating turret with a crossbow shooter and a crane. It also has its own jail cell, into which the ninja are thrown by the Dragon Hunters.

Set name	
Dieselnaut	
Year 2018	
Number 70654	
Pieces 1,179	
Minifigures 7	

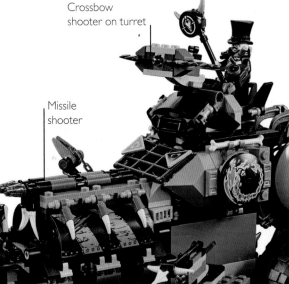

Missile shooter

Spear shooter

Snake shoulder armor

THE SECRETS OF THE FORBIDDEN SPINJITZU

The ninja have to call on all their skills when they are faced with a new set of fiery and icy foes. These include Aspheera, a flaming sorceress who seeks the weapons that once defeated her—the Scrolls of Forbidden Spinjitzu. As a result of her quest for revenge, Zane is sent to the frozen Ever-Realm. The ninja enter the realm, only to meet another villain in the form of the chilling Ice Emperor.

Cockpit decorated with golden swords

▲ ASPHEERA

Long ago, the Serpentine sorceress Aspheera got Master Wu to reveal the secrets of Spinjitzu to her. Yet before she could conquer Ninjago, Wu and Garmadon imprisoned her in a tomb for a thousand years. After being accidentally freed by the ninja, Aspheera uses her magic to steal Kai's fire powers. She then plots revenge against Wu.

CHAR

Char is Aspheera's loyal assistant. The sorceress brings his mummified body back to life using burning fire.

Whip

PYRO WHIPPER

Aspheera applies her new fiery powers to a dead breed of Serpentine snakes. In doing so, she brings them back to life as Pyro Vipers such as Pyro Whipper.

Flag with serpent design

Armor covers shoulder and chest

PYRO DESTROYER

Pyro Destroyer is another Pyro Viper Aspheera uses to help carry out her dastardly deeds. He is often armed with a scimitar and a shield.

Set name	
Fire Fang	
Year	2019
Number	70674
Pieces	463
Minifigures	4

Snake's hood

Swooshing, rattling tail

Fire Fang is bound in chains

◀ FIRE FANG

After Aspheera escapes from her Pyramid tomb, she uses magical lava fires to create an enormous Serpentine snake called Fire Fang. As well as providing transport for Aspheera, the snake also helps attack the Monastery of Spinjitzu. The ninja quickly learn to avoid its fiery breath and rattling tail!

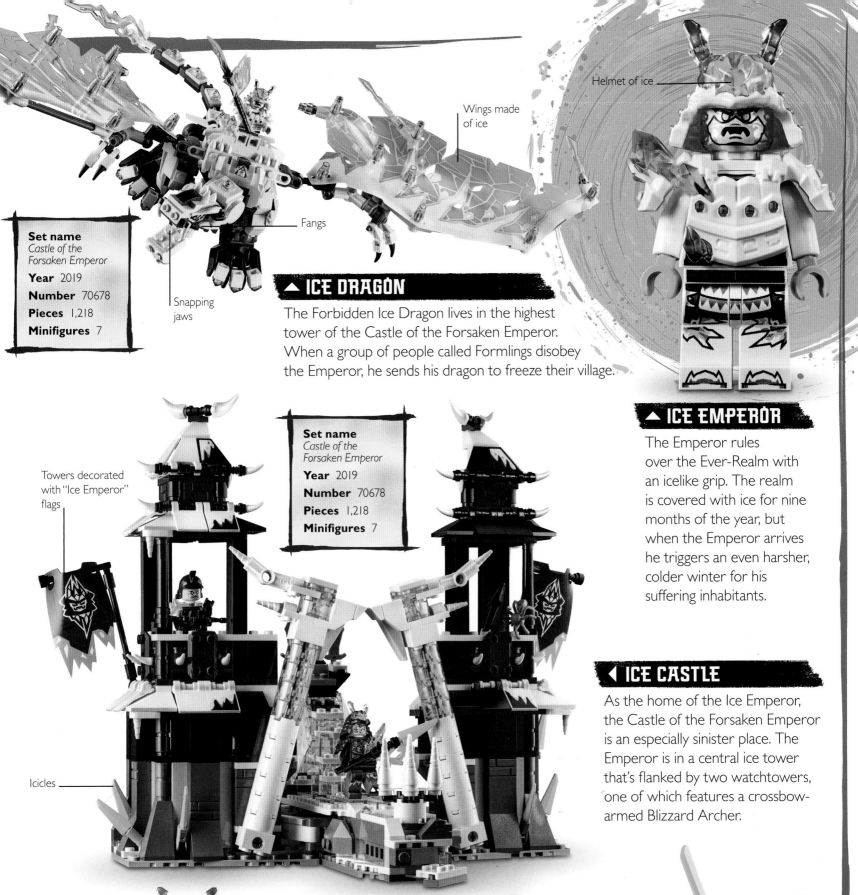

Set name
Castle of the Forsaken Emperor
Year 2019
Number 70678
Pieces 1,218
Minifigures 7

Snapping jaws

Fangs

Wings made of ice

Helmet of ice

▲ ICE DRAGON

The Forbidden Ice Dragon lives in the highest tower of the Castle of the Forsaken Emperor. When a group of people called Formlings disobey the Emperor, he sends his dragon to freeze their village.

▲ ICE EMPEROR

The Emperor rules over the Ever-Realm with an icelike grip. The realm is covered with ice for nine months of the year, but when the Emperor arrives he triggers an even harsher, colder winter for his suffering inhabitants.

Towers decorated with "Ice Emperor" flags

Set name
Castle of the Forsaken Emperor
Year 2019
Number 70678
Pieces 1,218
Minifigures 7

Icicles

◀ ICE CASTLE

As the home of the Ice Emperor, the Castle of the Forsaken Emperor is an especially sinister place. The Emperor is in a central ice tower that's flanked by two watchtowers, one of which features a crossbow-armed Blizzard Archer.

Crest on samurai helmet

GENERAL VEX

Vex is the Ice Emperor's trusted general. He wears a dramatic samurai helmet and is protected by some serious armor.

BLIZZARD ARCHER

Blizzard Archer guards the Ice Emperor from his perch in the Castle of the Forsaken Emperor. His crossbow is always at the ready to attack any invaders.

Crossbow

BLIZZARD SWORD MASTER

Blizzard Sword Master is well armed with two impressive ice katana. Unlike most of his fellow Blizzard Samurai, he wears a conical hat rather than a helmet.

CHAPTER 3:
THE LEGO® NINJAGO® MOVIE™

LLOYD

Lloyd is just an average, everyday high school student—who's secretly a ninja superhero! His father is Lord Garmadon, the most evil super villain in Ninjago City. Lloyd's fellow students never let him forget it. Whenever Garmadon attacks the city, Lloyd's classmates blame him. Lloyd just has to live with it, but he knows he can always call on his friends and fellow ninja.

Black robes with green details

▲ LLOYD

It's hard for Lloyd. He will never win a popularity contest when his dad is a super villain. Lloyd wishes he could have a loving father, but instead he has to fight against Lord Garmadon. Another battle he has is not revealing to his school friends that he is one of the Secret Ninja Force!

Bowl of cereal

TEEN LLOYD

Like other kids, Lloyd enjoys wearing a hoodie and eating breakfast cereal. Yet unlike other boys, he has grown-up responsibilities.

Designs for Green Ninja Mech Dragon

Silver sword with gold tassel

MASKED LLOYD

When Master Wu tells the ninja they each have their own element, Lloyd is upset—green is not an element!

▼ GREEN NINJA MECH DRAGON

Lloyd prepares to battle his father in his Green Ninja Mech Dragon. This robotic beast has shooters mounted on its legs, and its sides open up to deploy hidden pop-out thrusters. If Garmadon isn't frightened of the dragon's weapons, he should be afraid of the creature's giant swooshing tail!

Set name *Green Ninja Mech Dragon*
Year 2017
Number 70612
Pieces 544
Minifigures 4

Removable golden sword

Hidden pop-out thrusters

Head can turn and rotate

Whipping tail

Leg-mounted shooter

Adjustable robot tongue

BRICK FACTS

The dragon in Green Ninja Mech Dragon (set 70612) is the second version of Lloyd's dragon. It was first introduced in the 2016 set, The Green NRG Dragon (set 70593).

COLE

Cole is brave, strong, and down to earth. No wonder he's the Earth Ninja! Cole is fond of music, and he even has built-in turntables installed in his mech. Though he makes the occasional wisecrack, he has great respect for his fellow ninja. Once Master Wu tells Cole of his elemental power, Cole realizes he can control stones, rocks, and even shockwaves.

Hair swept up in topknot

▼ QUAKE MECH

Cole's monstrous Quake Mech features gorillalike arms that are fully "armed" for battle—the mech's shoulders open up to shoot soundwave missiles! Inside the cockpit area, Cole plays music that passes through the mech's shoulder loudspeakers. It is effective in distracting any foes!

Quake Mech gorilla emblem

Shoulder opens to reveal soundwave-shooting missiles

Big wheel with huge tire

▲ COLE

Given the solemn black robes that Cole wears, it's no surprise that he is the most serious of the ninja. He is also the only ninja to wear a sleeveless top and wristbands. His fashion choices may be inspired by his love of music. One thing's for sure—Cole dances to the beat of his own drum!

Sleeveless top

Gripping hands

Boom box

Set name
Quake Mech
Year 2017
Number 70632
Pieces 1,202
Minifigures 5

TEEN COLE

When he's not a crime-fighting ninja, Cole is a regular student. At school, he wears street clothes and carries a boom box. Rock on!

MASKED COLE

Dressed in his ninja gi and face wrap, Cole springs into action. He carries his signature weapon—a hammer.

NYA

Nya is the fearless and dynamic Water Ninja. She can take charge of any situation and thinks of herself as the strongest ninja in the crew. When Nya's in high school, she's always accompanied by her beloved motorcycle. Nya is very focused and confident—the other ninja often look to her to call the shots.

Cloth armor

One of two katanas

▲ NYA

Nya is proud of her achievements as a ninja. She hopes that one day she will be as respected as her hero, the famous ninja Lady Iron Dragon. As the Water Ninja, Nya has the power to manipulate water. She can create floating water-spheres, and spray her enemies with water geysers.

Biker jacket

MASKED NYA

Nya dons her armor-covered gi to join the other ninja and help Lloyd save Ninjago.

TEEN NYA

When she's in school, Nya wears a jacket and jeans. She looks just like any other student.

▲ TRAINING NYA

Nya must practice if she is to master Spinjitzu. When training, she wears white robes that are different from her ninja gi. Nya practices hard to become a true Spinjitzu Master!

Flag

Water cannon

Hose

Cockpit and controls

Self-adjusting knee joint

Set name
Water Strider
Year 2017
Number 70611
Pieces 494
Minifigures 4

▲ WATER STRIDER

Water Strider is Nya's mech. Its four spiderlike legs are surprisingly nimble, enabling this mech to climb anywhere. It also boasts lots of firepower in six missile shooters right below the cockpit. Nya and the other ninja are now ready to face Garmadon's thugs.

Suction feet

KAI

Kai is compassionate, loyal, and protective. He has a fiery spirit, which is why it's fitting that he's the Fire Ninja. Enthusiastic, chatty, and fond of hugs, Kai is a good friend to the other ninja and a good brother to Nya. However, he can be hotheaded, especially when Master Wu tries to teach him patience. Kai gets especially fired up when Garmadon attacks Ninjago City!

Serious facial expression

▶ FIRE MECH

Master Wu doesn't want his students to rely on their mechs, but Kai loves using his armored robotic suit. The Fire Mech has flamethrowers for hands, while flame disks also shoot out from the mech's shoulders. It's an effective machine to help defend Ninjago against the Shark Villains.

Heat shield

▲ KAI

As the Fire Ninja, Kai can create fire out of thin air. His spiky, reddish-brown hair looks like a fiery beacon. Kai's protective nature makes him distrust Lord Garmadon when the super villain tries to make a truce with the ninja.

Fire tank connected to arm

Set name
Fire Mech
Year 2017
Number 70615
Pieces 944
Minifigures 6

Flame from flamethrower

Gelled hair for a messy look

Face cage

Foot protected by heat shield

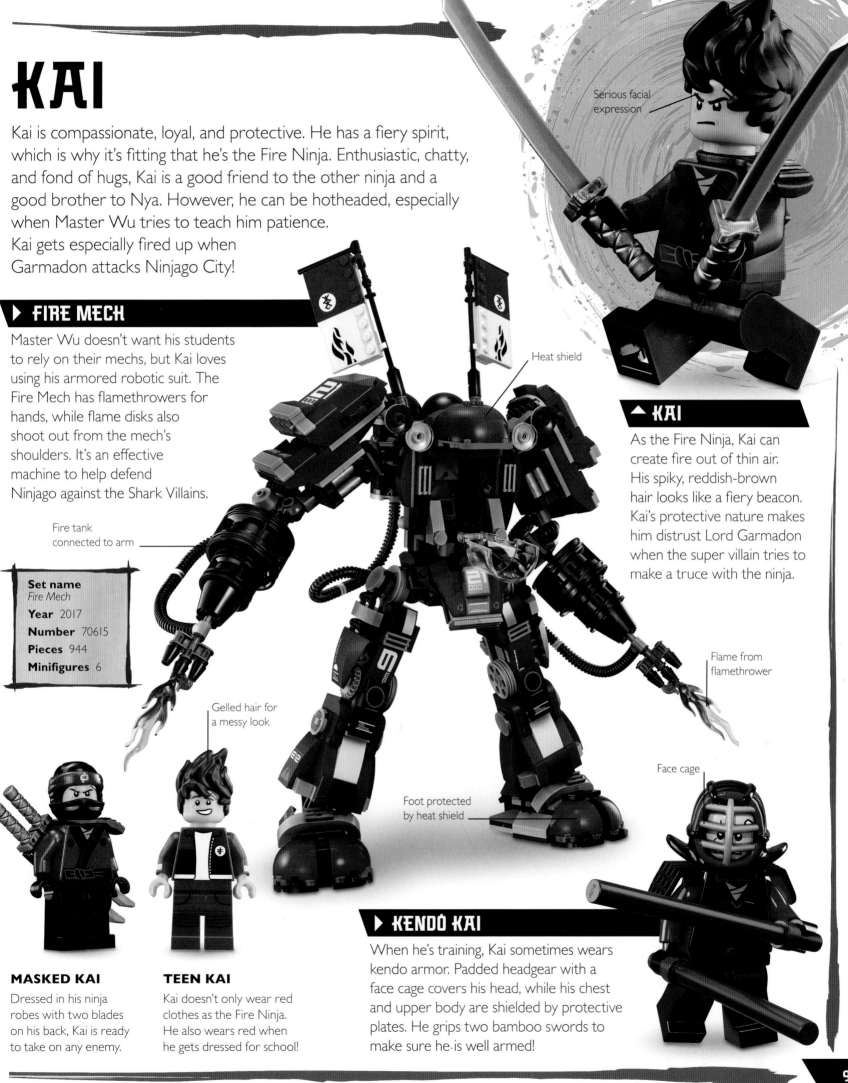

MASKED KAI

Dressed in his ninja robes with two blades on his back, Kai is ready to take on any enemy.

TEEN KAI

Kai doesn't only wear red clothes as the Fire Ninja. He also wears red when he gets dressed for school!

▶ KENDO KAI

When he's training, Kai sometimes wears kendo armor. Padded headgear with a face cage covers his head, while his chest and upper body are shielded by protective plates. He grips two bamboo swords to make sure he is well armed!

JAY

Jay is the Lightning Ninja, able to project bursts of lightning from his fingertips. He has a good heart, but his shyness can sometimes hold him back. However, the ninja are Jay's friends, and they are understanding. Jay shows his kindness by being the first of the ninja to comfort Lloyd when he tells them how upset he is that his father, Lord Garmadon, is a super villain.

Electric-blue belt

TEEN JAY

Jay also chooses blue when he dresses for high school. He loves a selfie opportunity—say "ninja!"

▲ JAY

The blue details on Jay's costume represent the the electric-blue color of lightning. Jay often doesn't speak unless he is spoken to. He has a crush on Nya, but whenever he tries to tell her how he feels, he gets interrupted!

Apron

EDNA WALKER

Edna is Jay's mother. One of her favorite things to do is collect seashells. Jay uses this as an example when telling Lloyd that everyone has their own unusual habits!

Pliers

ED WALKER

Ed Walker is Jay's father and Edna's husband. Ed likes to fix things, which is clear from the various tools hanging out of his overalls. Jay has a very close relationship with his parents.

Headband

MASKED JAY

Jay may be a little nervous, but he's also committed to being a ninja. If only the other kids at school knew how cool Jay looked in his ninja face wrap and robes!

Lightning rod

Rotating electro-disk

Bubble canopy

Lightning

▶ LIGHTNING JET

Jay's high-tech, jet plane-shaped mech can adjust its wings to execute difficult maneuvers. The Jet's spinning electro-disk generates electrical energy, while its cannon is effective against Garmadon's Shark Villains.

Set name	Lightning Jet	
Year 2017		**Number** 70614
Pieces 876		**Minifigures** 6

Landing strut

ZANE

Zane is literally super cool. As the Ice Ninja, he can zap his opponents with an icy blast. As he says, "Ice is nice!" Zane is a Nindroid—a robot that looks like a human—so he doesn't always understand the other ninja's humor or even how to be polite. He does try hard to fit in with the other ninja, and occasionally succeeds. Zane is a skilled ninja and supports his friends in the Secret Ninja Force.

Snow-white ninja gi

▼ ICE TANK

As they are both machines, Zane and his Ice Tank mech are physically connected—when Zane hops into the cockpit, his face briefly changes into a computer screen! The Ice Tank boasts huge tank treads that could easily flatten Garmadon's forces, though they are probably more afraid of the vehicle's ice cannon.

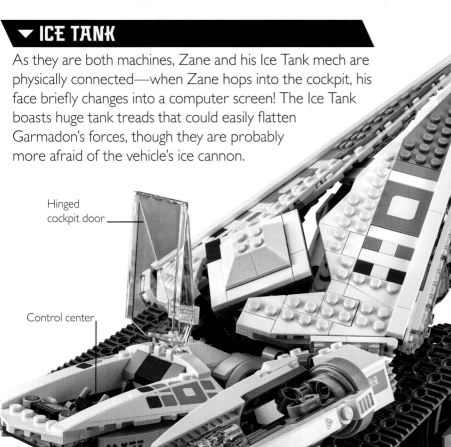

Hinged cockpit door

Control center

Ice cannon

Ice emblem on flag

Extra-wide tank tread

Set name	Ice Tank	
Year 2017	**Number** 70616	
Pieces 914	**Minifigures** 5	

▲ ZANE

Zane's signature weapon is the bow and arrow, and he keeps a quiver strapped to his back. A master of his bow, Zane hits his target every time.

POWERFUL ICE CANNON

The faster the mech moves, the faster its rotating ice chamber spins to produce ammunition that is fired out of a cannon next to the cockpit at the front. The chamber itself is positioned at the rear of the tank.

Rotating chamber

Festive winter sweater

TEEN ZANE

In day-to-day life, Zane tries hard to blend in. He dresses in clothes a human teenager would wear, and always tells jokes!

Cell phone

MASKED ZANE

Dressed in his full Ice Ninja outfit, Zane looks like the hero he is. When he's on missions, he can shoot ice projectiles from both his hands and feet to disarm his enemies.

NINJAGO® CITY AND DOCKS

Ninjago City is a modern metropolis on Ninjago Island where you will find mall-style buildings with a mix of shops, offices, restaurants, and homes. For example, this waterside, multi-level structure contains a movie theater, a comic book store, a tea shop, and an arcade. You'll find everything you need in Ninjago City—unfortunately, you will also find destructive super villains!

Radio tower

Puffer fish-shaped balloon

Sushi restaurant sign

Mannequin in clothing shop window

▶ CITY SCENE

The left side of this structure is a five-level complex, accessible by elevator. A fish market can be found on the lowest level, while the second floor features a crab restaurant. Lloyd lives on the top floor, which is also home to a rooftop sushi restaurant with a revolving sushi boat train!

Crab restaurant

ATM

Set name
NINJAGO® *City*
Year 2017
Number 70620
Pieces 4,867
Minifigures 19

BRICK FACTS

In terms of piece count, NINJAGO City was the largest NINJAGO set to date when it was released on September 1st, 2017. It was also the fourth-largest LEGO® set of all time.

In addition, even though Rufus MacAllister (aka Mother Doomsday) has been a recurring character since season 2 of LEGO NINJAGO: *Masters of Spinjitzu*, NINJAGO City is the first set to include his minifigure.

Water taxi phone

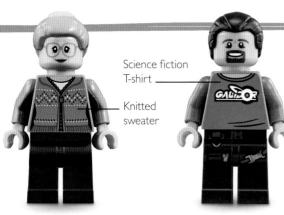

MYSTAKE

Mystake is the kind old lady who runs the tea shop near the docks in Ninjago City. You will always find her wearing a knitted sweater, and with her hair in a bun.

Knitted sweater

Science fiction T-shirt

RUFUS MACALLISTER

Rufus MacAllister, otherwise known as Mother Doomsday, works at the comic book store in Ninjago City. He is very knowledgeable!

Green jacket

MISAKO

Misako is Lloyd's mother. She was married to Lord Garmadon, but they had a falling out when Lloyd was a baby. As a Spinjitzu Master, Misako is a strong woman and a great mom!

DARETH

Dareth teaches martial arts at the Mojo Dojo and admires Lloyd and the other ninja. Dareth has slicked-back hair and wears a black ninja gi with gold details.

Freckles

LIL' NELSON

Lil' Nelson is a fan of the Secret Ninja Force. They're his heroes, and he hopes that they win against Garmadon's forces. He wears a white training outfit.

Pig balloon

▼ DOCK SCENE

The right side of this complex shows the back of Ninjago City's dockside area. Here you will find a sculptor's studio, Dareth's Mojo Dojo, and Mystake's Tea Shop. On the second floor, an arcade offers Ninjago City's residents the chance to play video games and buy bubblegum from a machine.

Set name	NINJAGO® *City Docks*
Year	2018
Number	70657
Pieces	3,553
Minifigures	14

Antennas

Retainer

NANCY

Nancy is one of the students at Lloyd's high school. She likes to gossip and has strong views—she's the first to point out that Lloyd's dad "ruins everything."

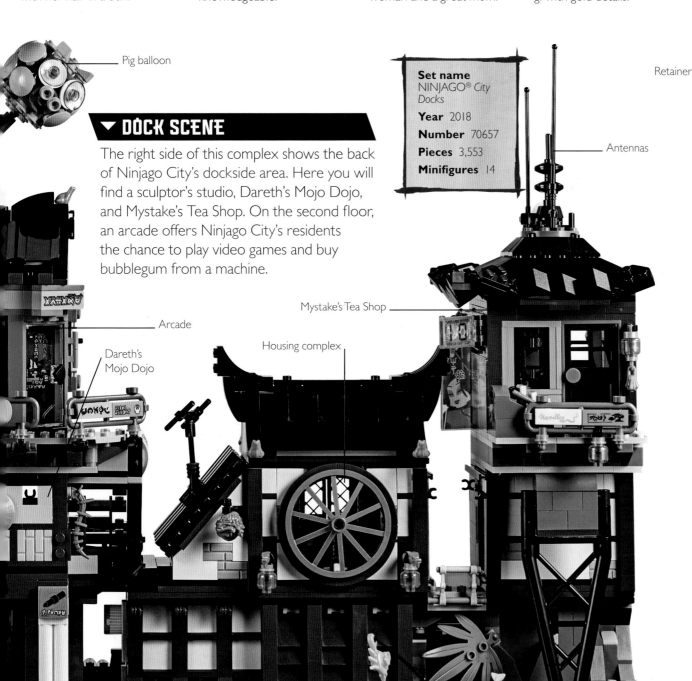

Arcade

Dareth's Mojo Dojo

Housing complex

Mystake's Tea Shop

CHAD

Chad is a cheerleader at Lloyd's high school. He's a mean boy, and he dislikes Lloyd so much that he makes up a song called "Boo Lloyd!"

UNDER ATTACK

Bustling Ninjago is a city of successful businesses, laughing children, and happy citizens—until Lord Garmadon and his Shark Villains attack! These fishy villains destroy buildings, panic customers, and scare little children. With this constant threat of chaos, no wonder the poor citizens of Ninjago are feeling gloomy.

Set name *garmadon, Garmadon, GARMADON!*

Year 2017

Number 70656

Pieces 830

Minifigures 6

Nomis

▶ POLICE TUK-TUK

When Lord Garmadon's army of nautical-themed henchmen marches into Ninjago City, Officer Toque hops into his Tuk-Tuk—a three-wheeled, motorized vehicle. The brave police officer wants to do what he can to protect innocent civilians. Soon, Toque is in hot pursuit of Garmadon's thugs.

Police sign

Siren

Single front wheel

Set name NINJAGO® *City Chase*

Year 2017 **Number** 70607

Pieces 233 **Minifigures** 5

▲ HOT DOG STAND

Nomis is serving a hot dog to a businessman when Garmadon appears in an enormous, high-tech, shark-shaped mech. The shocked businessman spits out the hot dog all over Nomis's outfit. Garmadon's invasion is not good for business—or for Nomis's cleaning bills!

NOMIS

Nomis runs a hot-dog stand in Ninjago City, though business suffers when Garmadon invades the city! Fun fact: Nomis and Lloyd share a birthday!

Light

Stall sign

Fresh fruit sign

Set name NINJAGO® *City Chase*

Year 2017

Number 70607

Pieces 233

Minifigures 5

◀ FOOD STALL

Ham is doing what he loves most—selling seafood and fresh fruit to the citizens of Ninjago City. However, disaster strikes when Garmadon's forces arrive and all Ham's potential customers run away in fright.

Dragons' heads at front of ship

► TAKUMA'S BOAT

Situated on an island, Ninjago City is a world of boats, canals, and waterways. Local fisherman Takuma is one of many people who make their living on the water. When he comes under aerial attack from Garmadon's goons, Takuma tries to protect his boat and the buckets of fish he has caught.

Set name
Flying Jelly Sub
Year 2017
Number 70610
Pieces 341
Minifigures 4

Small funnel

Flag

Warning light

Storage area

Buckets of fish

Hull of boat

Takuma

Set name
Destiny's Bounty
Year 2017
Number 70618
Pieces 2,295
Minifigures 7

Smaller sail at rear

Rickshaw canopy

► RICKSHAW

Ray makes his living by taking customers around Ninjago City in his rickshaw. Featuring a canopy and lanterns, the rickshaw is able to operate both day and night, in all types of weather. When Ninjago is overrun by Garmadon's Shark Villains, Ray is able to get his rickshaw out of the way of trouble.

Dragon on main sail

Ray pulls rickshaw

String of lanterns

Set name *Piranha Attack*
Year 2017   **Number** 70629
Pieces 217   **Minifigures** 4

◄ DESTINY'S BOUNTY

Destiny's Bounty is Master Wu's ship and the ninja's base. From here, they try to protect Ninjago City from Garmadon and other enemies. Facilities on the ship include a bedroom for Wu, a restroom, training dummies, and a dojo. If attacked, the ninja can access a secret weapon storage chamber filled with sai and katana.

Conical hat

Long, white beard

MASTER WU

Master Wu is an ancient ninja who has mastered the art of Spinjitzu. He is wise, patient, and kind. He is also very good at playing the flute! Master Wu is Garmadon's brother, but the two siblings haven't got along in a long time. When Master Wu falls into a river, the ninja think that this is the end for their beloved master. Fortunately, he returns on his ship, *Destiny's Bounty*!

◀ WISE WU

In his quest to teach the ninja to rely less on their mechs, Master Wu teaches them to practice Spinjitzu. His aim is for each of the ninja to become finely tuned fighting machines. This way, they won't need an enormous mechanized robot suit to win in a battle.

Set name *Master Falls*
Year 2017   **Number** 70608
Pieces 312   **Minifigures** 4

▼ JUNGLE BRIDGE

After Master Wu and Garmadon meet in the jungle, they fight on a rickety bridge. Garmadon falls over the edge, but Wu uses his staff to save him before trapping the super villain in a bamboo cage. When Wu then falls off the bridge into the river below, the ninja are in despair.

BRICK FACTS

The Master Wu minifigure in the complete LEGO® NINJAGO® MOVIE™ characters set (71019) comes with a very rare find—a box of corn flakes. It is the only cereal box to feature in a LEGO NINJAGO set.

CORN FLAKES

Bamboo cage

Wu's staff

Rickety bridge

Scorpion statues decorate the entrance

Set name *Spinjitzu Training*
Year 2017   **Number** 70606
Pieces 109   **Minifigures** 2

Kai is ready
to train

▲ DOJO WALL

The ninja visit Master Wu's dojo for some Spinjitzu training. A scroll decorates the wall of the training facility, which is also where two staffs—one with a claw on the end and the other featuring a fist—can be found.

▼ TEMPLE

After being told by Wu that the Ultimate Ultimate Weapon is on the other side of Ninjago Island, the ninja go in search of it. The brave heroes locate the weapon in a temple, though they need to beware—the building is filled with trap doors and booby traps.

Temple tower
with spire

Blue flame

Set name
Temple of the Ultimate Ultimate Weapon
Year 2017
Number 70617
Pieces 1,403
Minifigures 8

Scorpion
sculpture

Cage made
of bones

SPINJITZU TRAINING

Some of these items are found in Wu's dojo, while others are from the Temple of the Ultimate Ultimate Weapon.

TWO KATANAS

TRAINING STATION

SWORD RACK WITH KATANA

FIST AND CLAW STAFFS

BOOBY-TRAP BLADE

GARMADON COMBAT DUMMY

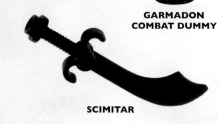

SCIMITAR

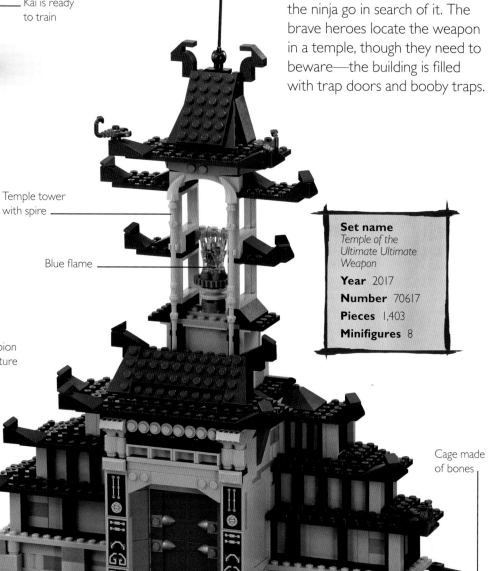

Large temple
doors open inward

LORD GARMADON

Lord Garmadon is a hard-working super villain who is desperate to conquer Ninjago City with his Shark Villains. The only thing standing in his way is Master Wu and his Secret Ninja Force. Yet unknown to Garmadon, the leader of the ninja is his own son, Lloyd. Garmadon isn't exactly a great dad—he doesn't even call Lloyd on his birthday! Soon, however, Garmadon starts rethinking his role as a father.

Sinister grin

▲ ROBE GARMADON

Wearing his armor and robes, Garmadon looks every bit the dark master. After he discovers that Lloyd is his son, Garmadon reaches out to him. The relationship is initially awkward, but father and son start to form an emotional bond.

Set name *Garmadon's Volcano Lair*

Year 2016

Number 70631

Pieces 521

Minifigures 5

Garmadon launches employees from here

Garmadon's personal armory

Lava flowing down side of volcano

▼ VOLCANO LAIR

Garmadon plans his schemes inside a volcano lair. The villain has stocked his base with everything he could want. The workshop has a cool robot arm and a launch pad with a clam-shaped drone aircraft. If any workers displease him, Garmadon shoots them out of the top of the volcano and into the air!

Robotic crane arm

Fish-shaped weapon

GIT
AUTHORIZED ACCESS ONLY

Computer lab

DANGER
MOVING PARTS

Explosive charge hidden in the wall

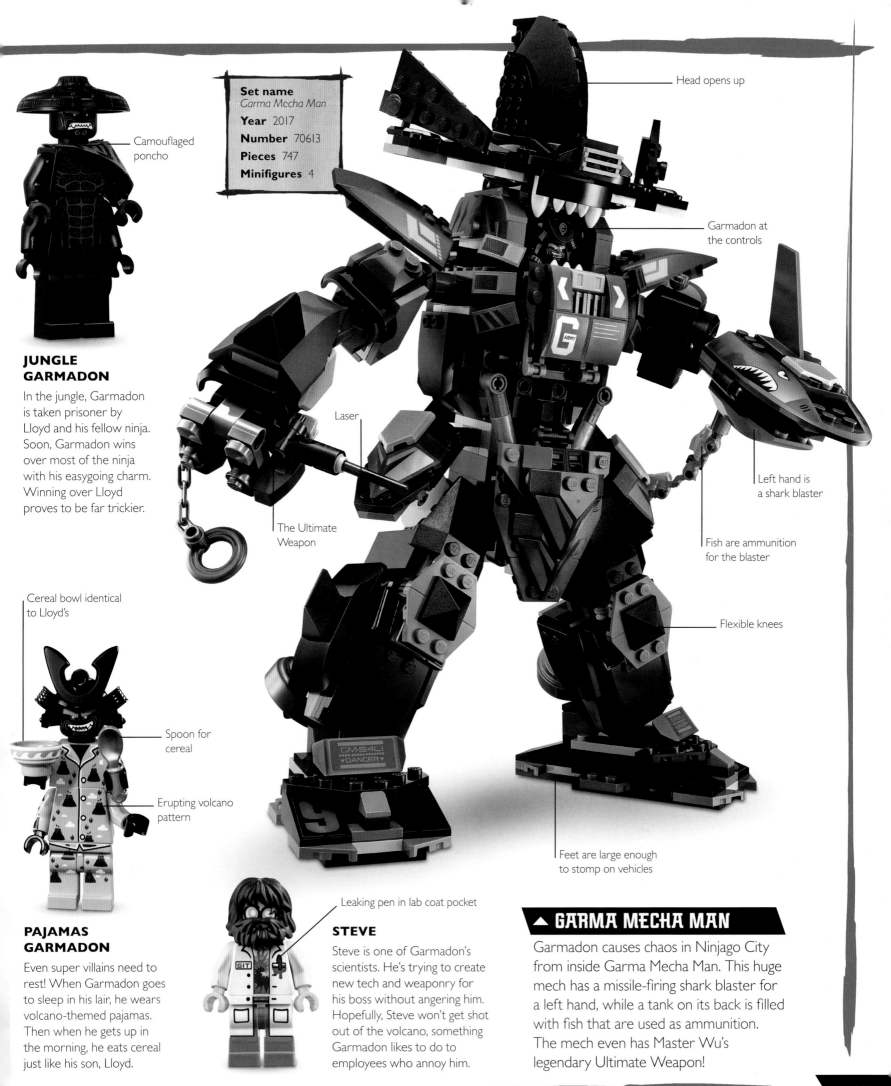

JUNGLE GARMADON

Camouflaged poncho

In the jungle, Garmadon is taken prisoner by Lloyd and his fellow ninja. Soon, Garmadon wins over most of the ninja with his easygoing charm. Winning over Lloyd proves to be far trickier.

PAJAMAS GARMADON

Cereal bowl identical to Lloyd's

Spoon for cereal

Erupting volcano pattern

Even super villains need to rest! When Garmadon goes to sleep in his lair, he wears volcano-themed pajamas. Then when he gets up in the morning, he eats cereal just like his son, Lloyd.

STEVE

Leaking pen in lab coat pocket

Steve is one of Garmadon's scientists. He's trying to create new tech and weaponry for his boss without angering him. Hopefully, Steve won't get shot out of the volcano, something Garmadon likes to do to employees who annoy him.

Set name *Garma Mecha Man*
Year 2017
Number 70613
Pieces 747
Minifigures 4

Head opens up

Garmadon at the controls

Laser

The Ultimate Weapon

Left hand is a shark blaster

Fish are ammunition for the blaster

Flexible knees

Feet are large enough to stomp on vehicles

▲ GARMA MECHA MAN

Garmadon causes chaos in Ninjago City from inside Garma Mecha Man. This huge mech has a missile-firing shark blaster for a left hand, while a tank on its back is filled with fish that are used as ammunition. The mech even has Master Wu's legendary Ultimate Weapon!

Periscope

Big glass "eye"

Rocket booster helps mech fly

SHARK VILLAINS

The Shark Villains help Lord Garmadon in his attempts to conquer Ninjago City. Their soldiers dress as sea creatures and use vehicles that resemble ocean life. Many generals have served as the Shark Villains' "General #1," but they don't last long—when the top general fails, Garmadon fires him out of his volcano. General #2 then steps up to become the new General #1!

▶ MANTA RAY BOMBER

You know that when Manta Ray Bombers are overhead, Garmadon is not far behind! This compact craft is armed with two missiles and two bombs. It is also very adaptable—if it falls to the ocean, the pilot can release the cockpit area, which becomes a raft for a swift escape!

Cockpit area turns into raft

Adjustable hinged wing

Set name *Piranha Attack*

Year 2017

Number 70629

Pieces 217

Minifigures 4

▲ PIRANHA MECH

The Piranha Mech is scary and unique, just the way Garmadon likes it! The mech's cockpit doubles as its lower jaw—when its mouth opens, a soldier can hop right in. A periscope provides an extra-high viewpoint, while twin missiles are positioned below the jaw.

Helmet shaped like a puffer fish

Set name *Manta Ray Bomber*
Year 2017   **Number** 70609
Pieces 341   **Minifigures** 4

Angler fish helmet

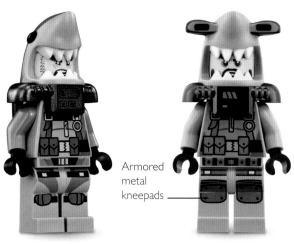

Armored metal kneepads

GREAT WHITE

Great White is the original General #1 of the Shark Villains. However, when he fails to correctly answer a question from Garmadon, the super villain ejects him from the volcano lair.

HAMMER HEAD

Hammer Head is the character who tries to cheer up Garmadon when he feels bad about Lloyd being mad at him. Then Hammer Head joins a line of dancers!

JELLY

Wearing a clear, jellyfish-like helmet, Jelly is another general who gets launched out of the volcano by Garmadon after the super villain fires the original General #1.

PUFFER

Puffer wears a dramatic head piece that really makes him stand out from the crowd. Purple in color, it features the large eyes and jagged spikes of a real pufferfish.

ANGLER

Just like a deep-sea anglerfish, this Shark Villains general has a head piece with sharp teeth and an unusual white lure at the top of his helmet.

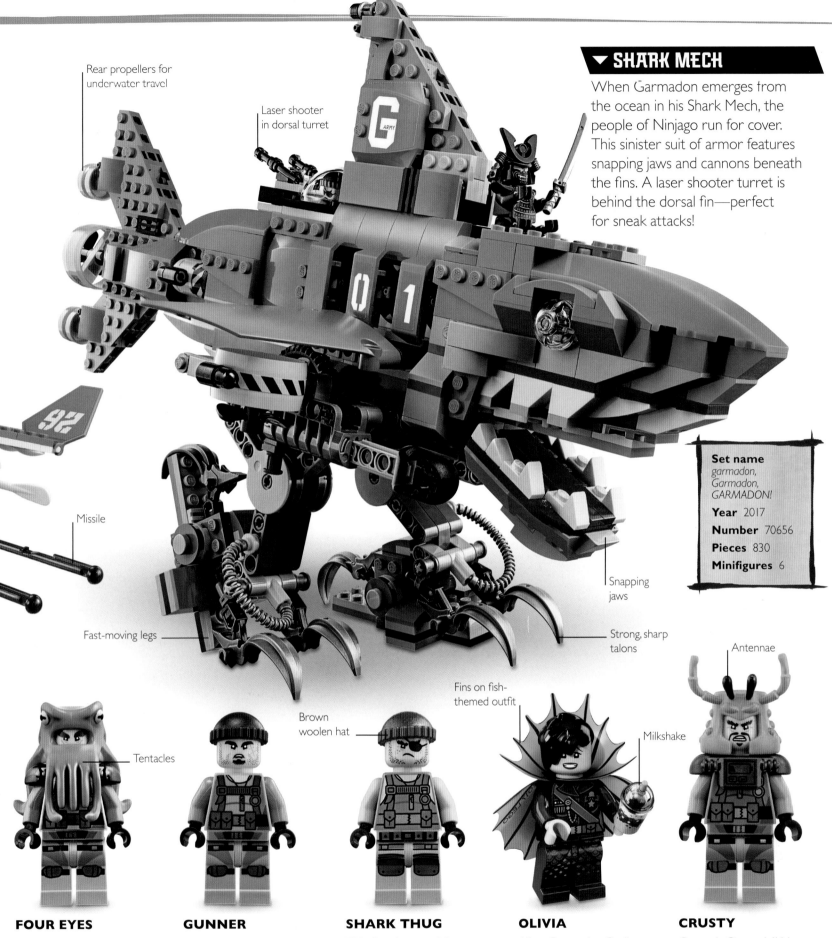

SHARK MECH

When Garmadon emerges from the ocean in his Shark Mech, the people of Ninjago run for cover. This sinister suit of armor features snapping jaws and cannons beneath the fins. A laser shooter turret is behind the dorsal fin—perfect for sneak attacks!

Rear propellers for underwater travel

Laser shooter in dorsal turret

Missile

Fast-moving legs

Snapping jaws

Strong, sharp talons

Antennae

Fins on fish-themed outfit

Brown woolen hat

Milkshake

Tentacles

Set name *garmadon, Garmadon, GARMADON!*

Year 2017

Number 70656

Pieces 830

Minifigures 6

FOUR EYES

While battling Garmadon's various generals, Lloyd confronts Four Eyes and pushes him aside. The tentacled soldier is so dazed, he has trouble getting back up!

GUNNER

Zane uses his ice powers to immobilize a platoon of Piranha Mechs. Piloting one of these mechs is Gunner, who's tossed from his mech during the battle.

SHARK THUG

This thug is one of the pilots leading the fleet of Manta Ray Bombers. When Jay blasts the bombers with lightning energy, the thug is thrown from his fish-themed airship.

OLIVIA

After Garmadon finally conquers Ninjago, Olivia becomes General #1. She soon gets fired out of the volcano lair, and sets up a colony in the jungle with other former generals.

CRUSTY

Crusty is General #6 in Garmadon's Shark Villains. When Garmadon invades, he orders Crusty and his men to take over the police station with their Crab Mechs.

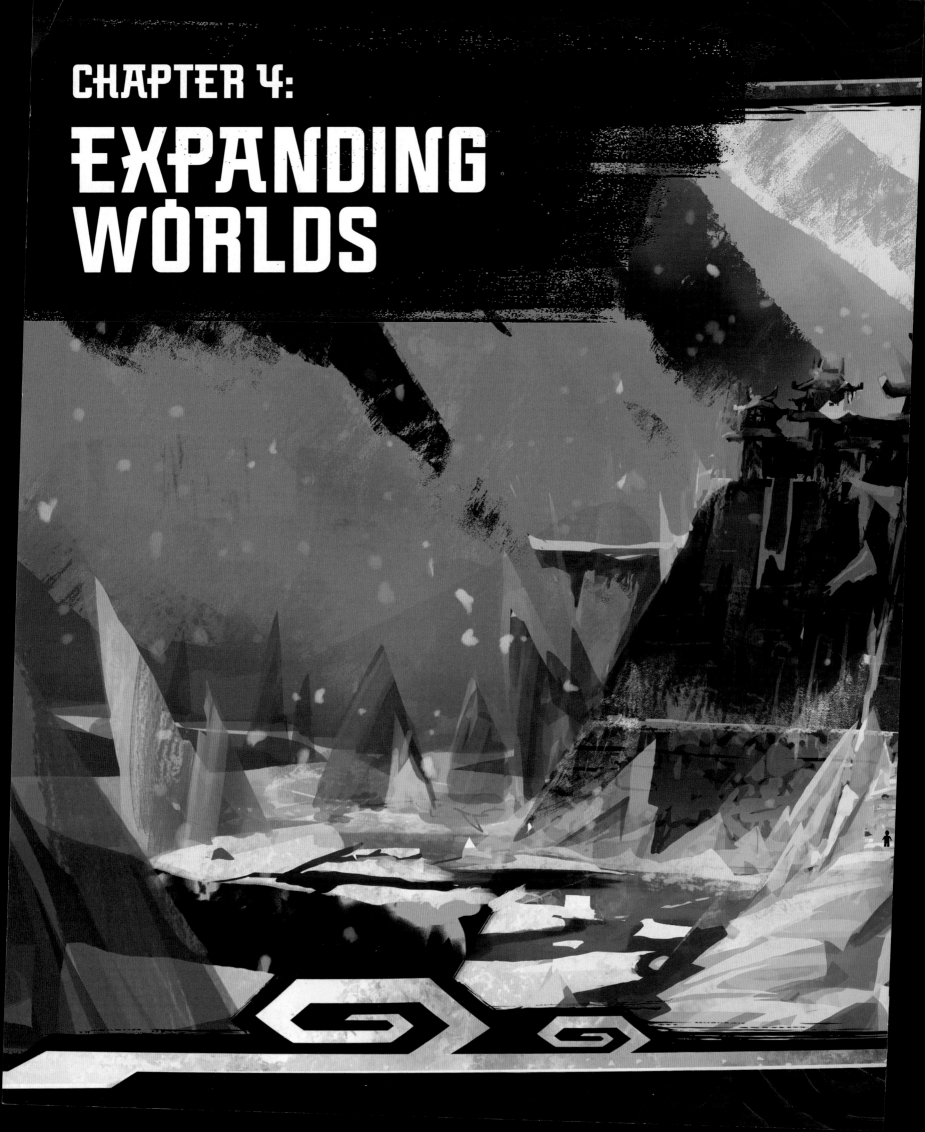

CHAPTER 4:
EXPANDING WORLDS

SPINJITZU

Spinner Sets have been at the heart of the LEGO® Ninjago world ever since it was created. The aim of the two-player Spinjitzu Spinners game is to knock the opposing character off their spinner. With unique sets released for the ninja, their friends, and enemies, players can take on the role of their favorite characters and battle against each other. For fans, it's as close to being in Ninjago as it gets!

Super bolt

Set name *Lloyd ZX*
Year 2012
Number 9574
Pieces 23
Minifigures 1

Crown

Fire Ninja symbol

Set name *Kai*
Year 2011
Number 2111
Pieces 19
Minifigures 1

◀ FIRST SPINNER

Kai's minifigure was the first to appear in a Spinner Set. The set contains his fiery orange spinner and three weapons to do battle with: a golden katana, a double-bladed dagger, and a spear.

Spinner

▲ SPINNER CROWN

Dressed in his ZX robes, Lloyd stands proud as the Green Ninja. He must now master Spinjitzu and battle the Serpentine tribes. The set includes a gold spinner, green crown, golden weapon, two regular weapons, four battle cards, and a character card.

▼ AIRJITZU BATTLE GROUNDS

The Battle Grounds are where players can train to be Spinjitzu Masters! The arena is also full of obstacles and challenges, with trapdoors on the rooftops and a collapsing staircase. In addition, the columns flanking the temple doors are removable launchers.

Ripcord

Set name *Airjitzu Battle Grounds*
Year 2016
Number 70590
Pieces 666
Minifigures 5

Trapdoor

Set name *Airjitzu Cole Flyer*
Year 2015
Number 70741
Pieces 47
Minifigures 1

▲ AIRJITZU

The ghostly version of Cole in this 2015 Airjitzu Flyer looks focused and ready for action. Among the many ninja weapons in the set are Cole's cleaver, swords, golden shurikens, and even a Sausage of Strength!

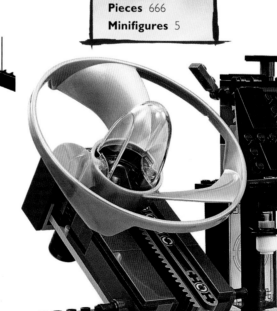

Removable Airjitzu launcher

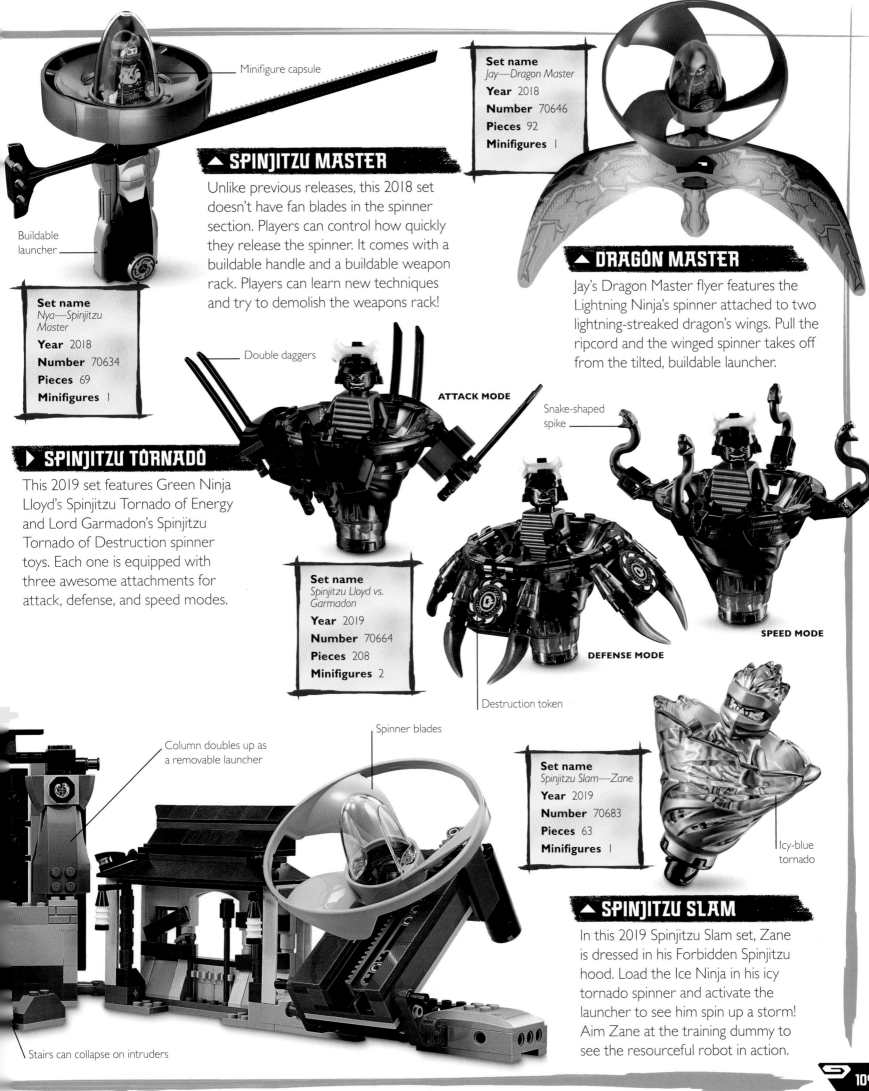

Minifigure capsule

▲ SPINJITZU MASTER

Unlike previous releases, this 2018 set doesn't have fan blades in the spinner section. Players can control how quickly they release the spinner. It comes with a buildable handle and a buildable weapon rack. Players can learn new techniques and try to demolish the weapons rack!

Buildable launcher

▶ SPINJITZU TORNADO

This 2019 set features Green Ninja Lloyd's Spinjitzu Tornado of Energy and Lord Garmadon's Spinjitzu Tornado of Destruction spinner toys. Each one is equipped with three awesome attachments for attack, defense, and speed modes.

Double daggers

ATTACK MODE

▲ DRAGON MASTER

Jay's Dragon Master flyer features the Lightning Ninja's spinner attached to two lightning-streaked dragon's wings. Pull the ripcord and the winged spinner takes off from the tilted, buildable launcher.

Snake-shaped spike

Destruction token

DEFENSE MODE

SPEED MODE

Column doubles up as a removable launcher

Spinner blades

Icy-blue tornado

▲ SPINJITZU SLAM

In this 2019 Spinjitzu Slam set, Zane is dressed in his Forbidden Spinjitzu hood. Load the Ice Ninja in his icy tornado spinner and activate the launcher to see him spin up a storm! Aim Zane at the training dummy to see the resourceful robot in action.

Stairs can collapse on intruders

TV SERIES

LEGO NINJAGO: *Masters of Spinjitzu* is an animated TV series based on the LEGO® NINJAGO® sets. The show begins at the moment the ninja are united as a team under Master Wu. It explores the history of Ninjago, the heroes' friendships, and their many exciting enemy encounters on the way to becoming fully-fledged ninja.

PILOT EPISODES

The pilot episodes and six mini-movies released online make up the pilot season of LEGO NINJAGO: *Masters of Spinjitzu*. They introduce Master Wu and his new ninja recruits—Cole, Jay, Kai, and Zane—as they search for four powerful Golden Weapons. When Kai's sister, Nya, is kidnapped by the Skulkin Warriors, the ninja use their training to defeat them. The ninja then realize that Master Wu's old enemy, Lord Garmadon, is behind the kidnapping. Garmadon escapes the Underworld, but plans to someday possess all four Golden Weapons.

SEASON 1: RISE OF THE SNAKES

The ninja meet Lord Garmadon's young son, Lloyd, who unleashes the ancient Serpentine tribe on Ninjago. Pythor, leader of the Serpentine, plans to bring back a mythic snake called the Great Devourer. The ninja have to protect Lloyd once it's discovered that he is the Green Ninja, the legendary warrior destined to defeat the Dark Lord in an epic confrontation. Eventually, the ninja have to get help from Garmadon to destroy the Great Devourer. Garmadon disappears with the four Golden Weapons that he needs to take control of Ninjago.

SEASON 2: LEGACY OF THE GREEN NINJA

The ninja train Lloyd so that he can face his father in battle. Garmadon converts all four Golden Weapons into the ultimate Mega Weapon. Using it, he goes back in time and tries to prevent the ninja from ever becoming ninja. The ninja follow Garmadon into the past and stop him. Garmadon's body is taken over by the Overlord, who faces Lloyd in the final battle. Lloyd unlocks his new powers and becomes the Golden Ninja, destroying the Overlord. In doing so, he pushes the evil out of his father's body, leaving a kindhearted Master Garmadon.

SEASON 3: REBOOTED

The ninja discover that the Overlord still exists in digital form in the virtual Digiverse created by Cyrus Borg. The Overlord plans to escape the Digiverse—he controls Borg's mind, summons an army of Nindroids, and enters the physical world. Lloyd gives up his Golden Power to prevent the Overlord from taking it and becoming the Golden Master. In outer space, the ninja try to stop the Nindroids from getting the Mega Weapon, but they fail. The Overlord becomes the Golden Master and, after attacking Ninjago, is destroyed by Zane. Did Zane himself survive?

SEASON 4: TOURNAMENT OF ELEMENTS

The ninja receive an invitation to the Tournament of Elements on Master Chen's island. There, they find out that they're not the only descendants of the original Elemental Masters. They also discover that Zane is still alive. The ninja fight the other Elemental Masters in the tournament. They realize that Chen is stealing the competitors' powers, which he intends to use to transform his worshippers into Anacondrai Warriors. The tournament competitors and the ancient Anacondrai Generals unite to defeat Chen. Garmadon's efforts to help the ninja see him sent to the Cursed Realm.

SEASON 5: POSSESSION

Lloyd is possessed by the ghost of Wu's first student, Morro. While in control of Lloyd's body, Morro steals Wu's staff, which contains clues to finding the Tomb of the First Spinjitzu Master. There, he finds a mighty relic called the Realm Crystal. The ninja reach the tomb and save Lloyd. However, Morro escapes with the Realm Crystal and uses it to summon the terrifying Preeminent. After being trained by Wu to be a Master of Water, Nya is able to unlock her elemental power and create a tidal wave—which puts an end to Morro and the Preeminent.

SEASON 6: SKYBOUND

When an evil Djinn called Nadakhan escapes from the Teapot of Tyrahn, he reassembles his old pirate crew and they become Sky Pirates. The ninja are tested by Nadakhan's wish-granting powers—aside from Jay and Nya, they're all trapped in his Djinn Blade. Nadakhan wants to marry Nya, who looks like his long-lost love. When the Sky Pirates mutiny, Nadakhan is defeated with poison, which also touches Nya and kills her. Jay makes a final wish—that the Teapot was never found. The world resets to the beginning of the adventure, with Nadakhan still in the Teapot.

SEASON 7: THE HANDS OF TIME

An old enemy of Wu's named Acronix reunites with his brother Krux. Together they're known as the Hands of Time. Time Blades fall out of the sky—if Krux and Acronix get all four, they can rule the world. The Hands of Time force Kai and Nya to retrieve the final Time Blade. Now that they have all four, the Hands of Time travel back in time. The ninja follow them and save the past. But when they come back to the present, Wu sacrifices himself. Or does he? It seems as though Wu never came out of the Time Vortex. Where could he be?

SEASON 8: SONS OF GARMADON

A year after Master Wu's disappearance, the ninja are protecting the Ninjago Royal Family. The heroes are trying to stop a biker gang called the Sons of Garmadon from reviving Lord Garmadon using the power of the three Oni Masks. Eventually, Lloyd discovers that Harumi, the princess of the Royal Family, is the leader of the Sons of Garmadon. She collects all three masks and resurrects Lord Garmadon, who is now completely sinister. Lloyd and Nya retreat to figure out what to do next. Meanwhile, the other ninja wake up to find themselves in the Realm of Oni and Dragons.

SEASON 9: HUNTED

Following the disappearance of most of the ninja, Lord Garmadon has taken over Ninjago City. Lloyd and Nya gradually build a resistance force to fight back against the ruthless Garmadon. Meanwhile, the other ninja are stranded in the Realm of Oni and Dragons. They're helped by Master Wu, who is now a child after returning from the Time Vortex. The ninja are hunted down and captured by the Dragon Hunters. They are eventually released and travel back to Ninjago on dragons! Wu becomes an adult again, and he finds the fabled Dragon Armor that will help him get back home.

BEHIND THE SCENES

At the heart of every LEGO® NINJAGO® set is a talented team of writers, designers, artworkers, and modelmakers. The team members work together to take new ideas all the way through to the screen and set. Story editor Tommy Kalmar and designer Michael Svane Knap reveal the many creative processes involved in expanding the Ninjago world.

▶ MEET THE TEAM

At the LEGO Group headquarters in Billund, Denmark, the LEGO NINJAGO team produce the fantastic creations that make every set so special. Your favorite ninja, most fearsome enemies, craziest mechs, and coolest vehicles were all created by this skilled team.

One of the prototype versions of Kai's vehicle

BACK ROW (LEFT TO RIGHT): MARKUS ROLLBÜHLER, ANGEL GRAU BULLÒN, FRÉDÉRIC ROLAND ANDRE, ESBEN FLØE, DJORDJE DJORDJEVIC
MIDDLE ROW: DIMITRIOS STAMATIC, LEONARDO FRANCISCO LOPEZ, MICHAEL SVANE KNAP, LI-YU LIN, KJELD WALTHER SØRENSEN
BOTTOM ROW: ALFRED MARTIN CHARTERS, DANIEL VELARDEZ SEGURA, CERIM MANOVI

"DESIGN IS A PROCESS ... YOU DON'T NEED THE FINAL DESIGN IN THE FIRST STROKE"

Michael Svane Knap

◀ STARTING A NEW SERIES

Every NINJAGO series is filled with new characters, vehicles, and adventures. The TV story writers and the model designers work together from the very start to come up with exciting new ideas. Who are the bad guys? What vehicles will they drive? What weapons will they use? Once the concept of the season has been established and initial models have been created, the story is developed.

▼ MAKING SKETCHES AND MODELS

Armed with a list of possible creations, LEGO NINJAGO concept artists draw up ideas for minifigures and models. Various designs are sketched to help develop different styles before a decision is made on which drafts to turn into 3D models. These prototypes are a way to get an early overall feel about everything from large sets to vehicles, minifigures, and components. The first models using LEGO bricks are now assembled.

A "Blizzard" minifigure makes it from the sketchpad to a production set

Tommy Kalmar and Daniel Velardez Segura discuss the story around Kai's vehicle

Prototype wheels are compared with illustrations of the components

Preliminary sketches of "Ice Samurai" minifigures, which will later become "Blizzard" characters

LISTENING TO THE FANS

Knowing what their fans want is important to the LEGO NINJAGO team. They test the models, minifigures, and storylines at every stage to hear what the young fans think. Even after a set is released in the stores, the team check comments and reactions on social media to inform future sets.

"WE LISTEN A LOT TO WHAT FANS WANT TO SEE"

Tommy Kalmar

▼ BUILDING THE ICE CASTLE

A large set, such as the impressive Castle of the Forsaken Emperor, can take more than a year to create. After initial sketches are drawn, a small prototype is produced to test for colors, form, and proportions. Elements of the model are produced using a 3D printer. A full-size test model is then created to check out the set's working details—in this case the palace's opening function—before the model is ready to go into production.

Michael sketches some ideas for set details

An early, scaled-down model

A larger prototype model

The final Castle of the Forsaken Emperor set

"TRUE POTENTIAL IS NOT STATIC ... IT EXCEEDS WHAT WE DARE TO IMAGINE!"

Tommy Kalmar

▶ SPINNING FORWARD

It's not only models and minifigures that keep evolving. The Spinjitzu sets have developed from simple toys to advanced spinners that can be customized with attachments and now more closely reflect the characters in LEGO NINJAGO: *Masters of Spinjitzu*. It reflects how the Ninjago world is a true combination of the TV show, models, and action play.

Michael takes zane for a spin

"IT WAS MAGICAL WATCHING THE KIDS' REACTION TO THE NEW SPINNERS. THEY SAID IT WAS LIKE SEEING THE TV SHOW COME TO LIFE"

Michael Svane Knap

Spinjitzu Zane with attachments

▼ CELEBRATING TEN SEASONS

To mark the tenth season of LEGO NINJAGO: *Masters of Spinjitzu*, a series of Legacy sets were released in 2019. These were original NINJAGO models given a new design and updated. They included classic sets such as the Giant Stone Warrior and the never-before-released Monastery of Spinjitzu.

Legacy Edition of the Giant Stone Warrior

BUILDING FOR THE FUTURE

What does the future hold for LEGO NINJAGO? Your favorite ninja in exciting new adventures with brilliant characters, epic enemies, and the coolest sets. As Tommy says, "the team are always striving to create the best possible play and story experience that new kids and fans will love." The NINJAGO future looks as action-packed as ever.

"AS LONG AS THE STORIES AND MODELS STAY FRESH AND EXCITING, NINJAGO WILL LIVE ON!"

Michael Svane Knap

CHARACTER GALLERY

LEGO® characters come in three basic parts: the head, the torso, and the hips and legs. LEGO® NINJAGO® characters feature many variations, including the helmets and armor for the ninja and the snake heads and tails of the Serpentine. Some of the Skulkin characters have extra-large skulls, while the general style of all characters was updated in 2015 and 2018.

TRAINING KAI
(2011)

KAI DX
(2011)

KAI ZX
(2012)

KAI ZX
(2012)

KENDO KAI
(2012)

NRG KAI
(2012)

KAI KIMONO
(2013)

TECHNO KAI
(2014)

JUNGLE KAI
(2015)

KAI TOURNAMENT
(2015)

KAI STONE ARMOR
(2015)

KAI TECHNO ARMOR
(2015)

KAI DEEPSTONE
(2015)

KAI DEEPSTONE ARMOR
(2015)

KAI AIRJITZU
(2015)

JUNGLE KAI
(2016)

KAI DESTINY
(2016)

KAI HONOR
(2016)

KAI FUSION
(2017)

KAI FUSION ARMOR
(2017)

GOLDEN KAI
(2017)

KAI RESISTANCE
(2018)

KAI HUNTED
(2018)

SPINJITZU KAI
(2018)

DRAGON MASTER KAI
(2018)

KAI LEGACY
(2019)

KAI FS
(2019)

KAI ARMOR
(2019)

TRAINING JAY
(2011)

JAY DX
(2011)

JAY ZX
(2012)

KENDO JAY
(2012)

NRG JAY
(2012)

JAY KIMONO
(2013)

TECHNO JAY
(2014)

JUNGLE JAY
(2015)

JAY TOURNAMENT
(2015)

JAY DEEPSTONE
(2015)

JAY DEEPSTONE ARMOR
(2015)

JAY AIRJITZU
(2015)

JAY TOURNAMENT
(2016)

JAY DESTINY ARMOR
(2016)

JAY DESTINY PIRATE
(2016)

JAY STONE ARMOR
(2016)

JAY HONOR
(2016)

JAY HONOR ARMOR (2016)

| **JAY FUSION** (2017) | **JAY FUSION ARMOR** (2017) | **JAY RESISTANCE** (2018) | **JAY BLACK KENDO** (2018) | **JAY HUNTED ARMOR** (2018) | **SPINJITZU JAY** (2018) | **DRAGON MASTER JAY** (2018) | **JAY LEGACY** (2019) | **JAY FS** (2019) |

| **JAY ARMOR** (2019) | **TRAINING COLE** (2011) | **COLE DX** (2011) | **COLE ZX** (2012) | **COLE ZX ARMOR** (2012) | **KENDO COLE** (2012) | **NRG COLE** (2012) | **COLE KIMONO** (2013) | **TECHNO COLE** (2014) |

| **COLE TOURNAMENT** (2015) | **JUNGLE COLE** (2015) | **COLE TECHNO ARMOR** (2015) | **COLE DEEPSTONE ARMOR** (2015) | **COLE AIRJITZU** (2015) | **COLE RX** (2016) | **JUNGLE COLE** (2016) | **COLE DESTINY** (2016) | **GHOST COLE DESTINY** (2016) |

| **GHOST COLE DESTINY ARMOR** (2016) | **COLE STONE ARMOR** (2016) | **COLE HONOR** (2016) | **COLE FUSION** (2017) | **COLE FUSION ARMOR** (2017) | **COLE BLACK KENDO** (2018) | **COLE RESISTANCE** (2018) | **COLE HUNTED** (2018) | **SPINJITZU COLE** (2018) |

| **DRAGON MASTER COLE** (2018) | **COLE LEGACY** (2019) | **COLE FS** (2019) | **COLE ARMOR** (2019) | **TRAINING ZANE** (2011) | **ZANE DX** (2011) | **ZANE ZX** (2012) | **KENDO ZANE** (2012) | **NRG ZANE** (2012) |

| **ZANE KIMONO** (2013) | **TECHNO ZANE** (2014) | **ZANE RX** (2014) | **TECHNO ZANE ARMOR** (2014) | **ZANE STONE ARMOR** (2015) | **JUNGLE TITANIUM ZANE** (2015) | **ZANE DEEPSTONE ARMOR** (2015) | **ZANE AIRJITZU** (2015) | **ZANE HONOR** (2016) |

ZANE TOURNAMENT (2016)

ZANE DESTINY ARMOR (2016)

PRISONER ZANE DESTINY (2016)

ZANE HONOR (2016)

ZANE FUSION (2017)

ZANE HONOR (2017)

ZANE WU-CRU (2018)

ZANE RESISTANCE (2018)

ZANE HUNTED (2018)

SPINJITZU ZANE (2018)

SNAKE JAGUAR ZANE (2018)

DRAGON MASTER ZANE (2018)

ZANE LEGACY (2019)

ZANE FS (2019)

ZANE ARMOR (2019)

ECHO ZANE (2016)

TRAINING NYA (2011)

NYA SAMURAI X (2012)

NYA SAMURAI X 2.0 (2014)

NYA JUNGLE SAMURAI X 3.0 (2015)

NYA JUNGLE SAMURAI X (2015)

NYA SAMURAI X DESTINY (2016)

NYA DESTINY ARMOR (2016)

NYA DESTINY ARMOR (2016)

WATER NYA (2016)

NYA HONOR ARMOR (2016)

NYA AIRJITZU (2016)

NYA FUSION ARMOR (2017)

NYA HONOR (2017)

NYA RESISTANCE (2017)

NYA SAMURAI RESISTANCE (2018)

KABUKI NYA (2018)

NYA WU-CRU (2018)

NYA HUNTED (2018)

SPINJITZU NYA (2018)

NYA SAMURAI X LEGACY (2019)

NYA LEGACY (2019)

NYA FS (2019)

NYA ARMOR (2019)

SENSEI WU (2011)

SENSEI WU (2011)

SENSEI WU (2012)

SENSEI WU PEARL GOLD HAT (2012)

EVIL WU (2014)

SENSEI WU POSSESSION (2015)

SENSEI WU (2015)

SENSEI WU POSSESSION (2015)

SENSEI WU DESTINY (2016)

MASTER WU HONOR (2016)

MASTER WU FUSION
(2017)

BABY WU
(2018)

TEEN WU
(2018)

DRAGON MASTER WU
(2018)

TEEN WU
(2019)

MASTER WU LEGACY
(2019)

MASTER WU CAPE
(2019)

LLOYD GARMADON
(2012)

LLOYD ZX
(2012)

LLOYD ZX KIMONO
(2012)

GOLDEN NINJA LLOYD
(2013)

LLOYD TECHNO ARMOR
(2014)

LLOYD STONE ARMOR
(2014)

LLOYD DX
(2014)

LLOYD STONE
(2015)

LLOYD TOURNAMENT
(2015)

JUNGLE LLOYD
(2015)

LLOYD DEEPSTONE
(2015)

EVIL GREEN NINJA
(2015)

LLOYD DESTINY
(2016)

LLOYD DESTINY ARMOR
(2016)

LLOYD DESTINY
(2016)

LLOYD HONOR
(2016)

LLOYD AIRJITZU
(2016)

LLOYD FUSION
(2017)

LLOYD FUSION ARMOR
(2017)

LLOYD RESISTANCE
(2018)

LLOYD HUNTED
(2018)

LLOYD HUNTED
(2018)

LLOYD WU-CRU
(2018)

LLOYD WU-CRU
(2018)

SPINJITZU LLOYD
(2018)

GOLDEN NINJA LLOYD LEGACY
(2019)

LLOYD LEGACY
(2019)

LLOYD GARMADON
(2019)

LLOYD FS
(2019)

LLOYD ARMOR
(2019)

LORD GARMADON
(2011)

LORD GARMADON
(2012)

LORD GARMADON
(2013)

MASTER GARMADON
(2014)

MASTER GARMADON TOURNAMENT
(2015)

LORD GARMADON RESURRECTED
(2018)

LORD GARMADON LEGACY
(2019)

KRUNCHA
(2011)

BONEZAI
(2011)

BONEZAI
(2011)

CHOPOV
(2011)

CHOPOV
(2011)

CHOPOV
(2011)

SAMUKAI
(2011)

FRAKJAW
(2011)

FRAKJAW
(2011)

FRAKJAW
(2011)

FRAKJAW
(2011)

FRAKJAW
(2016)

KRAZI
(2011)

KRAZI
(2011)

KRAZI
(2016)

WYPLASH
(2011)

WYPLASH LEGACY
(2019)

NUCKAL
(2011)

SKELETON
(2015)

SKELETON
(2018)

SKULKIN WARRIOR
(2019)

SKULKIN WARRIOR LEGACY
(2019)

PYTHOR
(2012)

PYTHOR LEGACY
(2019)

PYTHOR WHITE
(2015)

PYTHOR WHITE
(2016)

FANGTOM
(2012)

FANGDAM
(2012)

FANG-SUEI
(2012)

SNAPPA
(2012)

SKALES
(2012)

SLITHRAA
(2012)

MEZMO
(2012)

RATTLA
(2012)

ACIDICUS
(2012)

LIZARU
(2012)

SPITTA
(2012)

SPITTA LEGACY
(2019)

LASHA
(2012)

LASHA LEGACY
(2019)

CHOKUN
(2012)

SNIKE
(2012)

SKALIDOR
(2012)

BYTAR
(2012)

GENERAL KOZU
(2013)

GENERAL KOZU
(2016)

STONE SWORDSMAN
(2013)

STONE SWORDSMAN
(2013)

STONE SWORDSMAN
(2016)

STONE WARRIOR
(2013)

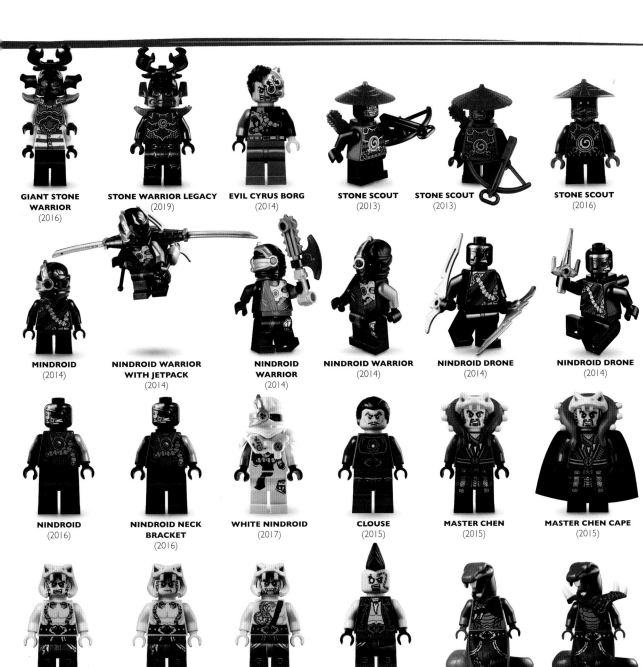

GIANT STONE WARRIOR (2016)

STONE WARRIOR LEGACY (2019)

EVIL CYRUS BORG (2014)

STONE SCOUT (2013)

STONE SCOUT (2013)

STONE SCOUT (2016)

STONE SCOUT (2019)

STONE SCOUT LEGACY (2019)

MINDROID (2014)

NINDROID WARRIOR WITH JETPACK (2014)

NINDROID WARRIOR (2014)

NINDROID WARRIOR (2014)

NINDROID DRONE (2014)

NINDROID DRONE (2014)

GENERAL CRYPTOR (2014)

GENERAL CRYPTOR (2016)

NINDROID (2016)

NINDROID NECK BRACKET (2016)

WHITE NINDROID (2017)

CLOUSE (2015)

MASTER CHEN (2015)

MASTER CHEN CAPE (2015)

ZUGU (2015)

KAPAU (2015)

SLEVEN (2015)

KRAIT (2015)

CHOPE (2015)

EYEZOR (2015)

KAPAU'RAI (2015)

CHOPE'RAI (2015)

EYEZORAI (2016)

MORRO (2015)

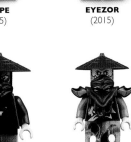

MORRO CAPE (2015)

GHOST WARRIOR GHURKA (2015)

GHOST WARRIOR WAIL (2015)

SCYTHE MASTER GHOULTAR (2015)

GHOST WARRIOR COWLER (2015)

GHOST WARRIOR PITCH (2015)

BLADE MASTER BANSHA (2015)

BLADE MASTER BANSHA GHOST (2015)

CHAIN MASTER WRAYTH (2015)

CHAIN MASTER WRAYTH GHOST (2015)

BOW MASTER SOUL ARCHER (2015)

BOW MASTER SOUL ARCHER GHOST (2015)

GHOST NINJA ATTILA (2015)

GHOST NINJA HACKLER (2015)

WOOO (2015)

HOWLA (2015)

CYREN BELT OUTFIT
(2016)

CYREN BELT OUTFIT SCABBARD
(2016)

CYREN DARK GREEN OUTFIT
(2016)

DOUBLOON
(2016)

DOUBLOON EPAULETS
(2016)

CLANCEE
(2016)

CLANCEE EPAULETS
(2016)

DADDY NO LEGS
(2018)

SQIFFY
(2016)

SQIFFY NECK BRACKET
(2016)

BUCKO
(2016)

FLINTLOCKE
(2016)

FLINTLOCKE EPAULETS
(2016)

CAPTAIN SOTO
(2016)

BIG FIGURE DOGSHANK
(2016)

TAI-D
(2016)

NADAKHAN
(2016)

SKY PIRATE SCABBARD
(2016)

SKY PIRATE TURBAN
(2016)

SLACKJAW
(2017)

RIVETT
(2017)

TANNIN
(2017)

VERMIN
(2017)

COMMANDER BLUNCK
(2017)

COMMANDER RAGGMUNK
(2017)

GENERAL MACHIA
(2017)

YOUNG KRUX
(2017)

KRUX—TIME TWIN YOUNG
(2017)

ACRONIX—TIME TWIN OLD
(2017)

LUKE CUNNINGHAM
(2018)

BIKER
(2018)

SKIP VICIOUS
(2018)

MR. E MASK OF VENGEANCE
(2018)

MR. E
(2018)

ULTRA VIOLET
(2018)

ULTRA VIOLET ONI MASK OF HATRED
(2018)

CHOPPER MAROON
(2018)

NAILS
(2018)

MOHAWK
(2018)

HARUMI QUIET ONE
(2018)

HARUMI
(2018)

HARUMI ONI MASK OF HATRED
(2018)

MUZZLE
(2018)

CHEW TOY
(2018)

JET JACK
(2018)

HEAVY METAL
(2018)

IRON BARON
(2018)

SKULLBREAKER
(2018)

ARKADE
(2018)

DRAGON HUNTER
(2018)

RONIN DEEPSTONE
(2015)

RONIN DEEPSTONE
(2015)

RONIN
(2016)

OVERLORD
(2014)

OVERLORD LEGACY
(2019)

P.I.X.A.L.
(2014)

P.I.X.A.L. SAMURAI X
(2017)

P.I.X.A.L. SAMURAI X
(2018)

PRISON GUARD
(2016)

MASTER YANG STATUE
(2015)

MASTER YANG
(2016)

GHOST STUDENT
(2016)

POSTMAN
(2015)

CLAIRE
(2015)

DARETH
(2015)

JESPER
(2015)

MISAKO
(2015)

SHADE
(2017)

NEURO
(2017)

GRIFFIN
(2016)

KARLOF
(2016)

ASH
(2017)

RAY
(2017)

MAYA
(2017)

SKYLOR
(2015)

SKYLOR HUNTED
(2018)

FUTURE JAY
(2018)

HUTCHINS
(2018)

LIL' NELSON
(2016)

AUTO
(2015)

NINJAGO TRAINING DROID
(2016)

ASPHEERA
(2019)

PYRO DESTROYER
(2019)

PYRO SLAYER
(2019)

CHAR
(2019)

PYRO WHIPPER
(2019)

ICE EMPEROR
(2019)

GENERAL VEX
(2019)

BLIZZARD WARRIOR
(2019)

BLIZZARD ARCHER
(2019)

BLIZZARD SWORD MASTER
(2019)

WOLF
(2019)

AKITA
(2019)

MOVIE CHARACTERS

THE LEGO® NINJAGO® MOVIE™ is packed with a fantastic range of characters, some familiar—though seen in different guises—and others introduced especially for the feature. This gallery includes standard minifigures from the movie as well as some harder-to-find collectible models.

LLOYD

TEEN LLOYD

MASKED LLOYD

MASKED LLOYD SLEEVE MARKINGS

KAI

TEEN KAI

MASKED KAI

MASKED KAI ARMOR

COLE

MUSIC COLE

MASKED COLE

MASKED COLE CUFFS

ZANE

MASKED ZANE

NYA

TEEN NYA

MASKED NYA

JAY

MASKED JAY

MASTER WU

LORD GARMADON

ROBE GARMADON

JUNGLE GARMADON

MISAKO

LADY IRON DRAGON

ED WALKER

EDNA WALKER

DARETH

LIL' NELSON

GENERAL #1

STEVE

GREAT WHITE

HAMMER HEAD

FOUR EYES

ANGLER

JELLY

CRUSTY

PRIVATE PUFFER

PUFFER

MIKE THE SPIKE

GUNNER

THUG

THUG SLEEVES	THUG STRIPED LEGS	OFFICER TOQUE	OFFICER NOONAN	HAM	PAT	LAUREN	HENRY
TORBEN	PATTY KEYS	JUNO	GUY	RUFUS MACALLISTER	TOMMY	JAMANAKAI VILLAGER	SALLY
IVY WALKER	SWEEP	KONRAD	SEVERIN BLACK	RAY	FRED FINLEY	NANCY	NOMIS
RUNME	CHAD	RUNJE	CHAN KONG-SANG	BETSY	RUNDE	MYSTAKE	TAKUMA

COLLECTIBLE MINIFIGURES

KENDO KAI	TEEN LLOYD	TEEN COLE	TEEN ZANE	TRAINING NYA	TEEN JAY	MASTER WU CEREAL BOX	MISAKO BAG	GREAT WHITE ARMED	GARMADON
SUSHI CHEF	PAJAMAS GARMADON	FLASHBACK GARMADON	ANGLER ARMED	OLIVIA	GPL TECH	GONG AND GUITAR ROCKER	SWORD LLOYD	N-POP GIRL	SHARK VILLAINS OCTOPUS

INDEX

Main entries are highlighted in bold.
Sets are listed by their full name.

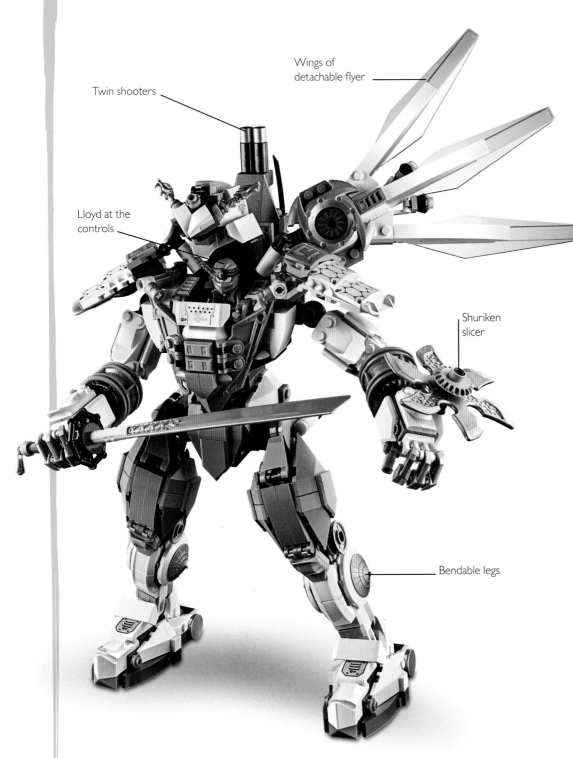

Wings of
detachable flyer

Twin shooters

Lloyd at the
controls

Shuriken
slicer

Bendable legs

LLOYD'S TITAN MECH

Senior Editor Phil Hunt
Senior Designer Lauren Adams
Editor Beth Davies
Designer Ray Bryant
Pre-Production Producer
Siu Yin Chan
Senior Producer Lloyd Robertson
Managing Editor Paula Regan
Managing Art Editor Jo Connor
Publisher Julie Ferris
Art Director Lisa Lanzarini
Publishing Director Simon Beecroft

This American Edition, 2019
First American Edition, 2014
Published in the United States by DK Publishing
1450 Broadway, Suite 801, New York, NY 10018

Page design copyright © 2019 Dorling Kindersley Limited
DK, a Division of Penguin Random House LLC
19 20 21 22 23 10 9 8 7 6 5 4 3 2 1
001–312824–Sept/2019

DK books are available at special discounts when purchased in
bulk for sales promotions, premiums, fund-raising, or educational
use. For details, contact: DK Publishing Special Markets, 1450
Broadway, Suite 801,
New York, NY 10018

SpecialSales@dk.com

Printed and bound in China

A WORLD OF IDEAS:
SEE ALL THERE IS TO KNOW

www.dk.com
www.LEGO.com

ACKNOWLEDGMENTS

Dorling Kindersley would like to thank Randi Kirsten Sørensen, Heidi K. Jensen, Paul Hansford, Martin Leighton Lindhardt, Tommy Kalmar, Michael Svane Knap, and the LEGO NINJAGO team (Cerim Manovi, Markus Rollbühler, Angel Grau Bullòn, Frédéric Roland, Andre Esben Fløe, Djordje Djordjevic, Dimitrios Stamatis, Leonardo Francisco Lopez, Li-Yu Lin, Kjeld Walther Sørensen, Alfred Martin Charters, Daniel Velardez Segura) at the LEGO Group for their invaluable help with making this book; Gary Ombler for his photography; Brian Poulsen for additional photography; James McKeag and Toby Truphet for additional design assistance; Nicole Reynolds and Pamela Afran for additional editorial assistance; Megan Douglass and Julia March for proofreading; and Helen Peters for the index.

PICTURE CREDITS
All images supplied by the LEGO Group
except: p.7 center left, Image courtesy of
LEGOLAND® California Resort.